When Lomax awakened, the past and the present had become so mixed that it was difficult to make sense of either.

Who am I, he thought? The Nightcomer on his mission of seventeen years ago, or Hugh Lomax, residence California, scriptwriter and novelist of sorts? There was no answer or none that would suffice. He had become a stranger to himself and he got to his feet and moved across to the wash-stand. As he started to dry himself, there was a knock at the door and Katina entered.

She was wearing the same silk headscarf and cream linen dress, and she closed the door and smiled. "How do you feel?"

He grinned. "Too old for street brawls with men half my age. It's a dangerous game to go back into the past."

Katina took out a clean shirt and handed it to him. "They say one should never return to any-thing," she offered.

"I'm beginning to think they're right. I'm not even sure who I am anymore."

"You are Hugh Lomax," she said, and with uncanny perception added, "The Nightcomer died a long time ago."

"I'm not so sure," he said. "I'm not so sure."

THE DARK SIDE OF THE ISLAND

Jack Higgins

A FAWCETT GOLD MEDAL BOOK

Fawcett Publications, Inc., Greenwich, Connecticut

THE DARK SIDE OF THE ISLAND

THIS BOOK CONTAINS THE COMPLETE TEXT OF THE
ORIGINAL HARDCOVER EDITION.

A Fawcett Gold Medal Book reprinted by arrangement with
Harold Ober Associates, Inc.

ISBN 0-449-13826-7

Printed in the United States of America

10 9 8 7 6 5 4 3 2 1

CONTENTS

Book One: The Long Return

Book Two: The Nightcomer

Book Three: A Sound of Hunting

And this one for Ruth

Book One

The Long Return

1

On Kyros, nothing changes

Lomax lay on the narrow bunk in the airless cabin, stripped to the waist, his body drenched in sweat, and stared up at the stained and peeling ceiling.

Looked at long enough, it became a pretty fair map of the Aegean. He worked his way down from Athens through the Cyclades to the larger mass that was Crete, but where Kyros should have been there was only an empty expanse of sea. For some reason it made him feel curiously uneasy and he swung his legs to the floor.

He got up, splashed water into the cracked basin that stood beneath the mirror beside the bunk and washed the sweat from his body. His shoulders were solid with muscle, his body bronzed and fit, and somehow the ugly puckered scar of the old bullet wound beneath his left breast looked sinister and out of place.

As he dried himself, a stranger stared out of the mirror. A man with skin stretched tightly over prominent cheekbones and dark, sombre eyes that examined the world with a curiously remote expression he could no longer analyse, even to himself.

As he reached for his shirt, the cabin door opened and the steward looked in. "Kyros in half an hour, Mr. Lomax," he said in Greek.

The door closed behind him and for the first time Lomax was conscious of a faint stirring of excitement, a cold finger that seemed to touch him somewhere inside. He pulled on his linen jacket and went out on deck.

As he stood at the rail watching Kyros gradually rise

out of the sea, Captain Papademos emerged from the deck-house and paused beside him. He was heavily built and almost blackened by the sun, his face seamed with wrinkles.

He put a match to his pipe. "It's difficult in this heat haze, but if you look carefully you can see Crete in the distance. Quite a view, eh?"

"Something of an understatement," Lomax said.

"I've been everywhere a sailor *can* go," Papademos continued. "In the end I found I was only travelling in a circle."

"Aren't we all?" Lomax said.

He took out a cigarette and Papademos gave him a light. "For an Englishman you speak pretty good Greek. The best I've heard from a foreigner. You've been out here before?"

Lomax nodded. "A long time ago. Before the flood."

Papademos looked puzzled for a moment and then his face cleared. "Ah, now I see it. You were in the islands during the war."

"That's right," Lomax said. "Working in Crete with the E.O.K. mostly."

"So?" Papademos nodded, serious for a moment. "Those were hard times for all of us. The people of these islands don't forget how much the English helped. Have you been back before?"

Lomax shook his head. "Never felt like it. In any case, I always seemed to have something more important to do. You know how it is."

"Life, my friend, she grips us by the throat." Papademos nodded sagely. "But seventeen years is a long time. A man changes."

"Everybody changes," Lomax said.

"Maybe you've got a point there, but why Kyros? I could think of better places."

"There are some people I want to look up if they're still around," Lomax said. "I'd like to see if they've changed too. Afterwards, I'll move on to Crete and Rhodes."

"On Kyros nothing changes." Papademos spat down into the water. "Ten years I've been making this trip and they still treat me as if I've got the plague."

Lomax shrugged. "Maybe they just don't like strangers."

Papademos shook his head. "They don't like anybody. You sure you've got friends there?"

"I hope so."

"So do I. If you haven't, you're in for a pretty thin time and you'll be stuck for a week until I call again."

"I'll take my chances."

Papademos knocked the ash from his pipe on the rail. "We'll be here for four hours. Why don't you have a quick look round for old times' sake and then go on to Crete with me? They'll show you a better time in Herakleion than they will here."

Lomax shook his head. "Next week I'll take you up on that offer, but not now."

"Suit yourself." Papademos shrugged and went back into the deck-house.

They were close inshore now, the great central peak of the island towering three thousand feet above them. As the little steamer rounded the curved promontory crowded with its white houses, a single-masted caicque, sails bellying in the breeze, moved out to sea. It passed so close to them that Lomax could see the great eyes painted on each side of the prow.

The man at the tiller waved carelessly and Lomax raised a hand and then the throbbing of the engines began to falter as they slowed to enter the harbour.

On the white curve of sand, brightly painted caicques were beached and fishermen sat beside them in small groups mending their nets while children chased each other in the shallows, their voices somehow muted and far away.

He went back to his cabin and started to pack. It didn't take long. When he was finished, he left the canvas grip and the portable typewriter on the bunk and went back on deck.

They were already working alongside the stone pier and as he watched the engines stopped and everything seemed curiously still in the great heat.

On the pier, three old men dozed in the sun and a young boy sat with a fishing line, a small black dog curled beside him.

As the steward emerged from the cabin carrying the canvas grip and the typewriter, Papademos came out of the deck-house. "You travel light."

"The only way," Lomax said. "What happens now? Do I just walk off the boat? Doesn't anyone want to see my papers?"

Papademos shrugged. "There's a police sergeant called Kytros who attends to all that. He'll know you're here soon enough."

By now a couple of sailors had the gangway in position. The steward went first and Lomax put on a pair of sunglasses and followed him.

As he took out his wallet to tip the man, he was aware that the three old men were all sitting up straight and looking at him curiously.

The boy who had been fishing was winding in his line. As the steward went back on board, he hurried across, the dog at his heels.

He was perhaps twelve with brown eyes in a thin, intelligent face. His jersey was too big for him and his pants had been patched many times.

He looked up at Lomax curiously for a moment and then said slowly in English, "You want a good hotel, mister? They look after American tourist real nice."

"What makes you think I'm an American?" Lomax asked him in Greek.

"The dark glasses. All Americans wear dark glasses." The boy replied in the same language instinctively and his hand went to his mouth in astonishment. "Say, mister, you speak Greek as good as me. How come?"

"Never mind that," Lomax said. "What's your name?"

"Yanni," the boy told him. "Yanni Melos."

Lomax extracted a banknote from his wallet and held it up. "All right, Yanni Melos. This is for you when we reach this hotel of yours where they treat Americans so well. It had better be the best."

Yanni's teeth gleamed in his brown face. "Mister, it's the only one in town." He picked up the canvas grip and typewriter and hurried ahead, the dog at his heels, and Lomax followed.

Nothing had changed. Not a damned thing. Even the pillbox the Germans had constructed to guard the pier was still standing, its concrete crumbling a little at the edges. All that was missing were the E-boats in the harbour and the Nazi flag over the town hall.

The boy led the way between tall, whitewashed houses, moving away from the waterfront. Once or twice they passed someone sitting on a doorstep, but on the whole, the streets were deserted.

The hotel formed one side of a tiny cobbled square with a church opposite. There were several wooden tables outside, but no sign of any customers, and Lomax guessed that the place would probably liven up in the evening.

He followed the boy into a large, stone-flagged room with a low ceiling. There were more tables and chairs and a marble-topped bar in one corner, bottles ranged behind it on wooden shelves.

Yanni put down the canvas grip and the typewriter and vanished through a door at the rear. It was cool and pleasant after the heat outside and Lomax leaned against the bar and waited.

He could hear a murmur of conversation and then a

girl's voice was raised, high and scolding. "Always you lie to me!" There was the sound of a slap and Yanni ran into the room head down, a young girl in a blue dress and white apron in hot pursuit.

She came to an abrupt halt when she saw Lomax and the boy made a dramatic gesture. "There, am I not speaking the truth?"

The girl was perhaps sixteen or seventeen, with a round, pretty face, and she came forward, wiping flour from her hands on the apron.

She stood looking at him helplessly, crimson with embarrassment, and Lomax smiled. "It's all right. I speak Greek."

Immediate relief showed on her face. "You must excuse me, but Yanni is such a liar and he caught me in the middle of baking. What can I do for you?"

"I'd like a room," he said. "Yanni told me this was the best hotel in town."

She looked as if she didn't know what to say and he added gently, "You do have one available, I take it?"

"Oh, yes," she assured him. "You've caught me rather by surprise, that's all. We seldom get tourists on Kyros. I'll have to get clean linen and air the mattress."

"Don't worry about that," he said. "There's no hurry."

He took a banknote from his wallet and handed it to Yanni. The boy examined it carefully and his eyes widened. He looked longingly at the open door, sighed and held out the note reluctantly.

"I think you've made a mistake, mister. It's too much."

Lomax closed the boy's hand over the note. "Let's call it an advance payment on your services. I may need you again."

Yanni's face split into a delighted grin. "Say, mister, I like you. You're my friend. I hope you stay on Kyros a long time."

He whistled to the dog and ran through the doorway

13

into the square. Lomax picked up the grip and the type-writer and turned to the girl.

"He is impossible," she said as she led the way out into a whitewashed passage.

"He seems to speak pretty good English?"

She nodded. "After his parents were drowned, he lived on Rhodes with his mother's people. I suppose he picked it up from the tourists."

"Who looks after him now?"

"He lives with his grandmother near the harbour, but she can't do much for him. She's too old."

They mounted narrow wooden stairs and turned into a corridor that seemed to run the full length of the building. She paused outside the door at the far end and said, "It's a very simple room. I hope you understand that?"

He nodded. "That's all I'm looking for."

She opened the door and led the way in. It was plainly furnished with a brass bed, a wash-stand and an old wardrobe. As elsewhere in the house, the walls were whitewashed and the wooden floor highly polished.

The whole place was spotlessly clean and he went and opened the window and looked out across the red-tiled roofs to the harbour below. "But this is wonderful."

When he turned, he saw that she was smiling with pleasure. "I am pleased you like it. How long will you be staying?"

He shrugged. "Until the boat comes again next week. Perhaps longer, I'm not sure. What do they call you?"

She blushed. "My name is Anna Papas. Would you like something to eat?"

He shook his head. "Not now, Anna. Later, perhaps."

She smiled awkwardly and retreated to the door. "Then I will leave you. If there is anything you need, anything at all, please call me. I will be in the kitchen."

The door closed behind her and he lit a cigarette and went across to the window.

Some fishing boats were moving in from the sea and

he could see the rusty little island steamer moored beside the pier. A gull cried as it swept across the rooftops and quite suddenly he was glad that he had returned.

2

A Man called Alexias

He unpacked his bag and then washed and shaved and put on a clean shirt. He was pulling on his jacket when the knock came at the door and a small, balding man entered.

He carried a stiff-backed ledger under one arm and smiled ingratiatingly, exposing bad teeth.

"Excuse me. I hope I'm not disturbing you?"

Lomax took an instant dislike to him, but he managed a smile. "Not at all. Come right in."

"I am the proprietor, George Papas," the little man said. "I'm sorry I wasn't here when you arrived. Mornings I work in my olive grove."

"That's all right. Your daughter looked after me fine."

"She is a good girl," Papas said complacently. He placed the ledger on the table by the window, opened it and produced a pen from the inside pocket of his jacket. "If you wouldn't mind signing the register. A legal requirement, you understand? The local police sergeant is fussy about such matters."

Lomax examined the book with interest. The last entry had been made almost a year before. He took the pen and entered his name, address and nationality in the appropriate columns.

"You don't seem to get many visitors here."

Papas shrugged. "Kyros is a quiet place with nothing much to attract the tourists—especially Americans."

"As it happens, I'm English," Lomax said. "Perhaps my tastes are simpler."

"English!" Papas frowned. "But my daughter assured me you were an American."

"A mistake the young boy who brought me here from the boat made," Lomax said. "I only live there. Does it matter?"

"No, of course not." Papas looked distinctly uncomfortable as he swivelled the register to examine the entry.

"Hugh Lomax—California," he mumbled. "Nationality English," and then his whole body seemed to be racked by a violent spasm.

For a moment, Lomax thought the man was about to throw a fit. He took his arm to lead him to a chair and Papas jerked it away as if he had been stung.

His face had turned a sickly yellow colour and his eyes were staring as he backed to the door.

"For God's sake, man," Lomax demanded. "What is it?"

Papas managed to open the door with one hand and crossed himself mechanically with the other. "Holy Mother of God," he breathed and stumbled into the corridor.

Lomax stood there for a moment, a frown on his face, and then picked up the register and followed him.

When he went into the bar, Anna was polishing glasses. She looked up and smiled. "Can I get you anything?"

He shook his head and placed the register on the bar. "Your father left that in my room by mistake. I'd like to have a word with him if I may."

"I'm afraid he's just gone out," she said. "I saw him crossing the square a moment ago."

"It can wait till later. Tell me, is there still a tavern on the waterfront called The Little Ship? It used to be owned by a man called Alexias Pavlo."

"It still is," she said. "Everyone knows Alexias. This year he is mayor of Kyros." She frowned in bewilderment. "But how could you know of Alexias and The Little Ship?"

"Remind me to tell you some time," he said, and went out into the bright sunshine.

As he crossed the square towards the street that led down to the harbour, Yanni emerged from it and ran towards him, the dog yapping at his heels He was wearing a scarlet shirt, khaki shorts and a pair of white rubber shoes.

He halted a few paces away, held out his arms and pirouetted. "Don't I look beautiful?"

"What's the idea?" Lomax said

Yanni spread his hands "If I'm working for such a rich and important man I must look the part These are my best clothes."

"That makes sense," Lomax said. "Where did you steal them from?"

"I didn't steal them," Yanni cried indignantly. "They were a present from a very good friend of mine The best friend I've got."

"All right," Lomax said. "Have it your way."

He moved down the cobbled streets towards the harbour and Yanni trotted beside him "Where do you want to go first?"

"A place called The Little Ship"

The boy's eyes widened. "You don't want to go there. That's a bad place. Not for tourists. For fishermen."

"Where would you suggest?" Lomax said.

"Lots of places. There's a Roman temple on the other side of the island, but we'd have to hire a boat. It's a long walk."

"Anything else?"

"Sure—the Tomb of Achilles, for instance."

"They buried him here, did they?"

Yanni nodded. "Everyone knows that."

"It must have been a long haul from Troy."

The boy ignored the remark. "We could always visit the monastery of St. Anthony or what's left of it. They blew it up during the war."

"So I'd heard," Lomax said, and his face darkened.

18

"Of course that would mean climbing the mountain. You'd probably find it too hot."

"That being so, I think we'll make it The Little Ship for the time being."

"Suit yourself." Yanni shrugged despondently and led the way along the waterfront.

The Little Ship was on the corner of a narrow alley and when they reached it, he hesitated at the entrance and turned appealingly. "Let me take you somewhere else, mister."

Lomax ruffled the boy's hair with one hand. "Don't look so worried." He grinned. "Shall I let you into a little secret? I've been here before. A long time ago. Before you were even thought of."

He turned from the boy's astonished gaze and went down the stone steps into the cool darkness of The Little Ship.

Just inside the entrance a young man sprawled in a chair against the wall and sang in a low voice, his fingers gently stroking the strings of a *bouzouki*.

He wore a red and green checked shirt, the sleeves rolled back carefully to display his bulging biceps to better advantage, and his hair curled thickly over the back of his collar.

He made no effort to move out of the way. Lomax stared down at him for a moment, anonymous in his dark glasses, and then stepped carefully over the outstretched legs and moved inside.

The first person he saw was Captain Papademos sitting by himself in a corner drinking red wine. Lomax raised a hand in greeting and Papademos deliberately looked away.

It was then that he became aware of a curious fact. There were six people in the room including Papademos, four of them sitting together and yet no one was talking.

The man behind the bar was small and wiry, his skin tanned the colour of Spanish leather. The right side of

19

his face was disfigured by an ugly scar and the eye was covered by a black patch.

He leaned on the bar holding a newspaper and completely ignored Lomax. The strange thing was that his hands trembled slightly as if he laboured under some terrible strain.

Lomax removed his sunglasses. "Is Alexias Pavlo about?"

"Who wants to know?" the man demanded in a hoarse voice.

"An old friend," Lomax said. "Someone from his past."

Behind him, the *bouzouki* player struck a final, dramatic chord. Lomax turned slowly and saw that everyone was watching him, even Papademos, and Yanni's white, frightened face peered round the edge of the door.

In the heavy silence, the whole world seemed to stop breathing and then a man stepped through the bead curtain that masked the door at the side of the bar.

In his time, he must have been a giant, but now the white suit hung loosely on his great frame. He moved forward slowly with a pronounced limp, leaning heavily on a walking stick, and the heavy moustache was iron grey.

"Alexias," Lomax said. "Alexias Pavlo."

Pavlo shook his head slowly from side to side as if he couldn't believe the evidence of his own eyes. "It *is* you," he whispered. "After all these years you've come back. When Papas told me, I thought he was insane. The Germans said you were dead."

The bead curtains parted again and George Papas moved out. There was sweat on his face and he looked frightened to death.

"It's me, Alexias," Lomax said, holding out his hand. "Hugh Lomax—don't you remember?"

Pavlo ignored the outstretched hand. "I remember you, Englishman." A muscle twitched at the side of his jaw. "How could I forget you? How could anyone on this island forget you?"

Suddenly, his face was suffused with passion. His mouth opened as if he wanted to speak, but the words refused to come and he raised his stick blindly.

Lomax managed to ward the blow off and moved in close, pinning Pavlo's arms to his sides. Behind him, a chair went over with a crash and Yanni screamed a warning from the door.

As he released Pavlo and started to turn, a brawny arm slid around his neck, half-choking him. He tried to raise his arms, but they were seized and he was dragged backwards.

The four men who had been sitting together held him in a vice half-way across their table. Papademos got to his feet and started for the door, but the man who had been playing the *bouzouki* shook his head gently and the captain sat down again.

The *bouzouki* player propped his instrument carefully against the wall and came forward. He looked down at Lomax for a moment, his expression perfectly calm, and then slapped him heavily in the face.

Lomax tried to struggle, but it was no use, and Pavlo pushed the *bouzouki* player out of the way. "No, Dimitri, he is mine. Lift up his head so that I can look at him properly.

Dimitri grabbed Lomax by the hair, pulling him upright and Pavlo looked into his face and nodded. "The years have treated you kindly, Captain Lomax. You look well—very well."

The little man with the scarred face and eye-patch had come from behind the bar and stood beside Pavlo and looked down at Lomax. Suddenly, he leaned forward and spat on him.

Lomax felt the cold slime on his face and anger boiled inside him. "For God's sake, Alexias. What's all this about?"

"It's really quite simple," Pavlo said. "It's about my crippled leg and Nikoli's face here. If you prefer it,

21

there's always Dimitri's father and twenty-three other men and women who died in the concentration camp at Fonchi."

And then it all began to make some kind of crazy sense. "You think I was responsible for that?" Lomax said incredulously.

"You were judged and condemned a long time ago," Pavlo told him. "It only remains for the sentence to be carried out."

He looked at the *bouzouki* player, his face like stone. "Give me your gutting knife, Dimitri."

Dimitri took a large clasp-knife from his hip pocket and passed it across. Pavlo pressed a button at one end and a six-inch blade, honed like a razor, sprang into view.

Lomax kicked out wildly, panic rising inside him. He made a last desperate effort and managed to tear one arm free. He swung round, dashing his fist into the nearest face, but in a moment, he was pinioned again.

The hand that held the knife trembled a little, but there was cold purpose in Pavlo's eyes. He took one pace forward, the knife coming up, and a voice said from the doorway, "Drop it, Alexias!"

Everyone turned and Lomax felt the grasp on his arms slacken. Standing just inside the door was a police sergeant in shabby sun-bleached khaki uniform, and Yanni peered under his arm.

"Stay out of this, Kytros," Pavlo said.

"I believe I told you to drop the knife," Kytros replied calmly. "I would not like to have to ask you again."

"But you don't understand," Pavlo told him. "This is the Englishman who was here during the war. The one who betrayed us to the Germans."

"So you would murder him now and in cold blood?" Kytros said.

Little Nikoli made an impassioned gesture with both hands. "It is not murder—it is justice."

"We obviously have different points of view." Kytros looked straight at Lomax. "Mr. Lomax, please come with me."

Lomax took a step forward and Dimitri grabbed his arm. "No, he stays here!" he said harshly.

Kytros unbuttoned the flap of his holster and took out his automatic. When he spoke there was iron in his voice. "Mr. Lomax is leaving with me now. I would be obliged, Alexias, if you would not make it necessary for me to shoot one of your friends."

Pavlo's face was contorted in anger and he half turned and drove the blade of the knife into the wooden table in a single violent gesture.

"All right, Kytros. Have it your way, but make sure he's on the boat when it leaves at four o'clock. If he isn't, I can't be responsible for what might happen."

Lomax stumbled past the sergeant and climbed the steps into the bright sunlight. For a moment, reaction set in and he leaned against the wall, his chest heaving as he struggled for breath.

Kytros put a hand on his shoulder. "Are you all right? Did they harm you?"

Lomax shook his head. "I'm getting a little too old to be playing that kind of game, that's all."

"Aren't we all, Mr. Lomax?" Kytros said. "My office is just around the corner. I'd be pleased if you would accompany me there."

As they walked along, Yanni tugged at Lomax's hand anxiously. "I got the sergeant for you, Mr. Lomax. Did I do right?"

Lomax smiled. "You saved my life, son. That's all."

Yanni frowned. "They say you're a bad man, Mr. Lomax."

"What do you think?" Lomax said.

The boy smiled suddenly. "You don't look like a bad man to me."

"Then we're still friends?"

"Sure we are."

They paused outside the police station and Lomax patted him on the head. "I'm going to be busy for a while, Yanni. You go back to the hotel and wait for me."

Yanni turned reluctantly and Lomax added, "It's all right. Sergeant Kytros isn't going to put me in prison."

The boy whistled to his dog and ran away along the waterfront and Lomax followed Kytros up the stone steps.

The sergeant led the way into an office furnished with a desk, several wooden chairs and a startlingly new green filing cabinet.

"The boy seems to have taken quite a fancy to you." He took off his cap and sat behind the desk. "It's a pity you won't be around longer. He could do with an improving influence."

Lomax pulled a chair forward and sat down. "So I'm definitely leaving, am I?"

Kytros spread his hands. "Mr. Lomax, be sensible. That could have been a nasty business back there at The Little Ship and I can't guarantee that it won't happen again. Alexias Pavlo is an important man on Kyros."

"Does that make him God?"

Kytros shook his head. "He doesn't need to be God to arrange for someone to slip a knife under your ribs one dark night."

"The Alexias Pavlo I knew seventeen years ago did his own killing," Lomax said.

Kytros ignored the remark. "Could I see your papers?"

Lomax produced them from an inside pocket and the sergeant examined them quickly. "What is the purpose of your visit to the island?"

Lomax shrugged. "I was here during the war. I thought I'd like to see the place again."

"But why Kyros, Mr. Lomax? The war must have taken you to many places."

"It happened to be the first port of call on the way from Athens," Lomax said. "It was as simple as that. I also intended to look up old friends in Crete and Rhodes. If I still have any, that is. After my reception here, I'm beginning to wonder."

"I see," Kytros passed the papers back. "These seem to be perfectly in order."

"What happens now?" Lomax asked.

"I should have thought that was obvious. You must leave on the boat at four o'clock."

"Is that an order?"

Kytros sighed. "Mr. Lomax, I notice that your visa has been franked by the minister himself. This means you have important friends in Athens."

"That's one thing you can count on," Lomax told him grimly.

"You place me in an impossible position," Kytros said. "If I force you to leave I will find myself in trouble in Athens. On the other hand, if you stay, someone will most surely try to kill you and I will again be to blame."

"But I must get to the bottom of this thing," Lomax said. "Surely you can see that? For a start, you can tell me why these people think I betrayed them to the Germans."

"Anything I know, I've heard at second-hand," Kytros said. "I'm from the mainland myself. I've only been here two years."

"Then what do you suggest?"

Kytros examined his wrist-watch. "You have exactly an hour and a quarter until the boat leaves. I would suggest that you go to the Church of St. Katherine and speak with Father John. He was here at the time in question."

Lomax looked at him in astonishment. "Do you mean Father John Mikali? But I met him when I was here during the war and he was at least seventy then."

"A very wonderful old man."

Lomax got to his feet and moved to the door. "Thanks for the advice. I'll see you later."

"On the pier at four o'clock," Kytros told him. "And remember, Mr. Lomax. Time is your enemy."

He pulled a sheaf of papers forward and reached for a pen and Lomax went outside and walked back along the waterfront.

3

Two Candles for St. Katherine

The lights in the little church were very dim and down by the altar the candles flickered and St. Katherine seemed to float out of the darkness bathed in a soft white light.

The smell of incense was overpowering and for a moment he felt a little giddy. It was a long time since he had been in a church and he stretched out a hand and touched the cold roughness of a pillar in the darkness to bring himself back to reality and moved down the aisle.

Father John Mikali knelt in prayer by the altar. His pure, almost childlike face was raised to heaven and in the candlelight the beard gleamed like silver against his dark robes.

Lomax sat on one of the wooden benches and waited and after a while the old priest crossed himself and got to his feet. When he turned and saw Lomax he showed no visible emotion.

Lomax got to his feet slowly. "A long time, Father."

"I was told you were here," Father John said.

Lomax shrugged. "News travels fast in a small town." The old priest nodded. "Especially bad news."

"You too?" Lomax said bitterly. "Now I know I'm in trouble."

"It is not for me to judge you," Father John said, "but it was foolish of you to return. Once the grass has grown over a grave it is not good to disturb it."

"All I want are the answers to a few questions," Lomax said. "If you of all people won't help me, who will?"

Father John sat down on one of the benches. "First, let *me* ask *you* a question. Why have you returned to Kyros after all this time."

Lomax shrugged. "An impulse, I suppose."

But there was more to it than that—much more. He squeezed his hands together and frowned, trying to get it straight in his own mind.

After a while he said slowly, "I think I came here looking for something."

"It would interest me to know what," the old man said.

Lomax shrugged. "I'm not really sure. Myself, perhaps. The man I lost back there in the past so many years ago."

"And you thought to find him here on Kyros?"

"But this was where he existed, Father. Don't you see that? During the past two or three years a strange thing's been happening to me. The events that other man was involved in here in these islands so many years ago seem more real to me than those things which have happened since. More important in every way. Does that make any kind of sense?"

The old priest sighed. "Captain Lomax, for these people that man has been dead for seventeen years. It would have been better if you had not resurrected him."

"All right, Father," Lomax said. "Let's get down to hard facts. The last view I had of Kyros was from the deck of the E-boat which was taking me to Crete after the Germans had captured me. What happened after I left?"

"Everyone who helped you was arrested," Father John said. "Including their immediate relatives. Some were shot in the main square as an example, the rest were sent to a concentration camp in Greece. Few survived the ill-treatment."

"And the people think I was responsible? That I betrayed them?"

"You were the logical person and the fact that the

Germans failed to execute you seemed to prove it. After all, they usually shot any British officer they caught who'd been working in the mountains with the Resistance."

"But that's ridiculous," Lomax said.

"You were badly wounded, perhaps even a little delirious. How can you be sure? In such a state, a man does strange things."

"Not a chance," Lomax said stubbornly. "I didn't talk, Father. Believe me."

The old man sighed. "It's painful to have to tell you this, but I can see that I must. Colonel Steiner made no secret of the fact that he had persuaded you to give him the information he needed in exchange for your life."

Lomax felt as if a cold wind had passed over his face. "But that isn't true," he said. "It can't be. I didn't tell Steiner a damn thing."

"Then who did, Captain Lomax? There *was* no one else. They were very thorough, you know. They even included me."

Lomax looked at him incredulously. "They arrested *you*?"

Father John smiled gently. "Oh, yes. I too sampled the delights of their concentration camp at Fonchi."

Lomax buried his face in his hands. "This thing's beginning to seem like a waking nightmare. Did you know that Alexias Pavlo actually tried to kill me a little while back?"

Pain flashed across the old man's face. "So it has started already? And violence breeds violence. This was what I was afraid of."

Lomax got up and paced nervously across the aisle. For a moment he stood there staring into space, a slight frown on his face, and then he turned quickly.

"If I'd really been guilty of this terrible thing do you think I'd have dared show my face here again, even after seventeen years? I know these islands and their people. I spent four years in the mountains with them. They

29

believe in an eye for an eye and they've the longest memories in the world."

"A good point," Father John said, "but it could be argued that the situation here has taken you by surprise. That you were not aware of what took place as a consequence of your action."

Lomax stood looking at him feeling curiously helpless and then weariness flooded through him in a great wave. He slumped down, his shoulders bowed in defeat. "For God's sake, what's the use?"

The old priest stood up. "Believe me, my son, I harbour no resentment against you, but I fear the evil that your presence here may produce. I think it would be better for all of us if you left on the steamer that brought you here. You still have time."

Lomax nodded. "Perhaps you're right."

Father John murmured a blessing. "I must go now. My presence in the streets may help to prevent any expression of violence when you leave."

He moved away along the aisle and Lomax stayed there on the bench, his head in his hands. He was past caring, his mind numb, gripped by a force he seemed unable to cope with. All the strength was draining out of him and he leaned forward and rested his head against a pillar.

Someone ran in through the entrance of the church and paused and then steps sounded on the stone flags of the aisle.

It was the perfume he first became aware of, strange and somehow alien in that place, like lilac fresh after rain, and it tingled in his nostrils bringing his head up sharply.

A young girl was standing there in the half-darkness, a scarf covering her head peasant-fashion. She was breathing heavily as if she had run a long way and she stood there staring down at him and no word was spoken.

His mouth went dry and something that was almost fear

moved inside him because this thing was not possible.

"Katina!" he said hoarsely. "Little Katina Pavlo."

She moved closer, a hand reaching out to touch his cheek and her face became that of a beautiful, mature woman in her middle thirties. In the candlelight it seemed to glow, to become alive.

"The Germans told us you were dead," she said. "That the boat in which they sent you to Crete was sunk."

He nodded. "It was, but I was picked up."

She sat down beside him, so close that he could feel the warmth of her thigh through her linen dress. "I was in one of the shops buying supplies when I heard you had come in on the steamer from Athens. I couldn't believe it. I ran all the way."

Her forehead was damp with perspiration and he took out his handkerchief and dried it gently. "It's not good to run in this hot sun."

She smiled faintly. "Seventeen years and still you treat me like a child."

"A moment ago I thought you still were. You made the heart move inside me, but it was only a trick of the candlelight."

"Have I changed so little, then?"

"Only to grow more beautiful."

Her nostrils flared and something glowed in the dark eyes. "I think you were always the most gallant man I ever knew."

For a moment time seemed to have no meaning, the present and the past merging into one. In some strange way it was as if they had sat here in the candlelight of the little church before, as if everything that happened was a circle turning endlessly upon itself.

He took her hand gently and said, "How did you know I was here?"

"Sergeant Kytros told me." She hesitated. "I heard what happened at The Little Ship. You must forgive my uncle. Sometimes I think he is no longer in his right

31

mind. He has lived with great pain for so many years."

"And he blames it all on me?"

She nodded gravely. "I'm afraid so."

"Along with everyone else around here, including Father John. Why should you be any different?"

"Because I know you sacrificed yourself for these people," she said calmly.

He laughed and the sound of it was harsh and ugly. "You try telling that one to Alexias and his pals and see how far it gets you."

"I did," she said. "A long time ago, but only one person would believe me."

He frowned. "Who was that?"

"Oliver Van Horn."

"They told me in Athens that he'd stayed on here after the war. I'd hoped to visit him. Does he still live in the villa out on the point?"

"I keep house for him."

His eyebrows arched in surprise. "You never married?"

She shook her head. "Never."

"He must be in his sixties now," Lomax said slowly.

The right-hand corner of her mouth twitched slightly and there was amusement in her eyes. "We have no arrangement, if that is what's worrying you."

"None of my business," he said, but he smiled for the first time and she smiled back. "How do the locals treat him these days? After all, *he's* English enough in all conscience."

"Not to the islanders. He suffered as much as anyone. He was taken with the rest of us."

Lomax frowned, a thought suddenly occurring to him for the first time. "And you, Katina? What happened to you?"

She shrugged. "They took me away with the others."

"To the concentration camp at Fonchi?"

She shook her head. "No, to another one, but they were all the same." She leaned forward and touched his face. "You look older. Too much older. I think you have been very unhappy."

He shrugged. "Seventeen years is a long time."

"Are you married?"

He hesitated briefly and then plunged straight in and it was surprising how easy it was now, almost as if he was talking about some distant relative or a casual friend who wasn't really important.

"I had a wife and a little girl. They were both killed in an automobile accident in Pasadena five years ago."

Her sigh echoed away into the darkness. "I knew there was something, but I wasn't sure. It still shows in the eyes." She took his hands and held them firmly. "Tell me now. Why have you come back to this place?"

"When Father John asked me, I told him I was looking for my other self," he said. "The one who existed here in these islands so many years ago, but now I'm not so sure."

"There is a deeper reason," she said. "Am I not right?"

"Who knows?" he shrugged. "Van Horn once told me that life was action and passion. If that's true, there's been precious little of either in mine for quite some time. Perhaps I thought I could recapture something."

"And what are you going to do now? Leave on the boat?"

"That's what they all seem to want me to do. Alexias told Kytros he wouldn't be responsible for what might happen if I stayed."

She glanced at her watch. "You would seem to have twenty minutes in which to make up your mind."

"What would *you* like to see me do?"

She shrugged. "It isn't my decision to make. It can only be your own."

She started to get to her feet and he held her hand and frowned, because he knew that for some strange reason this was the pivot on which the whole thing would turn.

"Do you want me to stay?"

"It would take courage," she said. "Very great courage."

He smiled suddenly. "But I gave *you* my courage a long time ago, remember?"

She nodded, her face serious. "I remember."

For a little while they sat there staring at each other and then she gently released his hand and stood up. "I'll only be a moment."

He watched her go down to the altar and drop to one knee, then she stood up, selected two candles and placed them under the statue of St. Katherine. It was only as she lit them with a taper that he realised who they were for and a lump came into his throat that threatened to choke him.

He got to his feet and walked blindly through the half-darkness to the door.

4

The Bronze Achilles

Outside in the square it was very hot and he stayed in the shade of the porch and smoked a cigarette as he waited for her.

Once, Anna appeared in the door of the hotel with a bucket and cloth as if intending to wipe down the outside tables, but at the sight of him, she drew back hurriedly.

It was quiet and deserted, the shadows long and black as the afternoon waned, and nothing stirred. He stood there, the cigarette burning between his fingers as he stared moodily out into the square and in some strange way it was as if he was waiting for something to happen.

There was a slight movement behind and he turned. Katina looked gravely up at him.

He smiled gently. "It was a long time ago."

Suddenly, there were tears in her eyes and he slipped an arm about her shoulders and held her close. They stayed there in the cool shadow of the porch for a little while and then she sighed and pushed him away.

"We must go. If you intend to catch that boat, you're running out of time."

He followed her out on to the steps, his mind in a turmoil. At that moment, Yanni staggered into the square from the street that led down to the waterfront.

His clothes were torn and covered in dust and his face was streaked with tears as he sobbed uncontrollably. In his arms, he held the little black dog.

Katina was already running to meet him and by the

time Lomax arrived, she was on her knees in front of the boy. "What is it, Yanni? What's happened?"

He held out the dog in his arms. Its head lolled to one side, the neck obviously broken, and there was froth on its mouth.

"It was Dimitri," he said. "Dimitri killed him."

"But why?" Katina demanded.

"Because I helped Mr. Lomax," Yanni sobbed. "Because I helped Mr. Lomax."

The rage that erupted inside Lomax was a searing flame that seemed to fuse with his whole being. He started forward and Katina said, "Hugh!"

When he turned, her face was very white, the eyes so dark a man could never fathom them.

"Be careful," she said. "He's already served two years in prison for manslaughter. When he's been smoking hashish, he doesn't know what he's doing."

He turned and walked quickly across the square and when he entered the street, he started to run. By the time he merged on the waterfront he was soaked in sweat and people turned to stare curiously at him.

This time he could hear no music coming from The Little Ship and he went straight down the steps without pausing and came to a halt just inside the door.

There were perhaps a dozen people sitting drinking and none of them had been there on his earlier visit. The man behind the bar was one of those who had held him across the table for Alexias. He was in the act of pouring wine into a glass and his mouth went slack in amazement.

Every head turned and Lomax examined the faces quickly and then crossed to the bar. "I'm looking for Dimitri."

The barman shrugged. "Why ask me? I'm not his keeper."

He picked up a glass and started to dry it with a soiled cloth and Lomax turned slowly and crossed the room.

Dimitri's *bouzouki* still leaned beside the chair where

he had left it and Lomax picked it up and smashed it against the wall in a single violent gesture.

He turned to face the room and no one moved. "I asked for Dimitri," he said calmly.

For a moment, they all sat there looking at him quietly, and then an old man with white hair and a moustache burned brown by tobacco said, "He is on the pier waiting to see you leave."

Lomax turned and went back up the steps into the hot sunlight. He crossed the road on the run and moved along the wharf.

The steamer was almost ready to leave and he could see Papademos up on the bridge leaning out of an open window, shouting down orders to the sailors on the pier as they started to loosen the mooring ropes.

There were perhaps two dozen people standing about in small groups. Alexias leaned against a pillar, a cigar between his teeth, and little Nikoli with the scarred face stood with him.

It was Nikoli who saw Lomax first and he tugged at the big man's sleeve and pointed and Alexias said something quickly and every head turned.

Half of them were young waterfront layabouts in brightly checked shirts, hair carefully curled over their collars. They were of a type to be found in every country in the world. Mean, vicious young animals who thrived on trouble.

One of them turned and made a remark and they all laughed and then Lomax saw Dimitri at the back of them. He was leaning against a windlass, a cigarette smouldering between his lips as he shaved a piece of wood with his gutting knife.

As Lomax approached, the crowd parted and he paused a couple of feet away from Dimitri. The *bouzouki* player was humming tunelessly to himself. He didn't even bother to raise his head.

Alexias moved forward, Nikoli at his side. "This is the

wrong time to seek trouble, Lomax. The boat leaves in five minutes."

Lomax turned very slowly and looked at him contemptuously. "When I want to hear from you I'll let you know. Once you were a man, but now . . ."

As he turned away, Dimitri reached to the cobbles for another piece of wood and Lomax kicked it out of his way.

Dimitri looked up slowly. His eyes were very pale, the pupils like pin-points. He still kept on humming to himself, but a muscle twitched spasmodically at one side of his jaw.

"With children and dogs you're quite a man," Lomax said clearly so that all could hear. "How about trying someone a little nearer your own size?"

One moment, the *bouzouki* player was lolling back against the windlass, the next he had moved forward, the knife cutting upwards like molten silver in the sunlight.

Lomax could have broken the arm with supreme ease. Instead, he pivoted and chopped down with the edge of his hand. Dimitri screamed, dropping the knife, and Lomax kicked it over the edge of the pier into the water.

He felt completely cool and without fear. It was as if that other, younger man had returned to take over. The one who had been trained to use such methods until they were a reflex action.

There was an ugly murmur from Dimitri's friends, but he held up a hand and shook his head. When he spoke, his voice was curiously remote and far away. "I'll break his neck as easily as I did the dog's."

All work had ceased on the ship and everyone waited. As Lomax circled warily, he saw people hurrying along the waterfront and then an old jeep appeared from a side street and braked to a halt and Katina and Yanni got out.

A segull cried harshly and swooped down and Dimitri

jumped in close, his right fist swinging in a tremendous punch.

To Lomax the blow seemed to travel in slow motion. He swerved slightly, allowing the *bouzouki* player to plunge past him, and slashed him across the kidneys with the edge of his hand.

Dimitri screamed and fell to the cobbles. For a little while he stayed there on his hands and knees and when he got to his feet, he was slobbering like an animal.

He lurched forward again and Lomax grabbed for his wrist with both hands and twisted it round and up so that he held him in a Japanese shoulder lock. Dimitri screamed again and still keeping that terrible hold in position, Lomax ran him head-first into a stack of iron-bound crates.

There was a gasp from the crowd and Lomax stood back and waited. Dimitri grabbed for a chain and heaved himself to his feet. When he turned, his face was a mask of blood. His hand slipped from the chain as he took one tottering step forward and collapsed.

There was a moment of stunned silence and then a spontaneous roar of anger from Dimitri's friends. As Lomax turned, they came forward with a rush.

He swung a fist into the first face and then a foot caught him on the shin and he cried out and started to sag. As he bent over, a knee lifted into his face and the cobbles rose to meet him.

He rolled desperately, face tucked into his shoulder, hands protecting his genitals, and then a shot echoed flatly across the water and then another.

It was as if all the clocks in the world had stopped at the same moment. Dimitri's friends moved back reluctantly and Lomax scrambled to his feet.

Father John Mikali stood a few feet away and Kytros was at his side, automatic in one hand, the other hooked into his belt. He looked very calm and completely in control.

Lomax stood there, his body aching, the taste of blood in his mouth, and Kytros said quietly, "The boat is waiting for you, Captain Lomax."

Lomax turned and looked at Alexias. On the big man's face was something that might almost have been respect, but there was more also. A slight frown of bewilderment as if for the first time he was unsure of himself and of the situation.

Lomax took a deep breath to clear his head and turned. He brushed past the sergeant and walked back along the pier and the people moved silently to each side.

From somewhere a thousand miles away he could hear Papademos shouting to his men and the rattle of the anchor chain and there was a roaring in his ears.

Katina was there, her arms around him and Yanni, his face white with excitement. She led him to the jeep and the boy opened the door and Lomax slumped into the passenger seat.

She climbed behind the wheel and leaned across to wipe blood from his face. "Are you all right?" she asked calmly.

He could feel her hand trembling and he held it for a moment and smiled. "A good thing Kytros arrived when he did. I'm getting a little old to be playing that kind of game."

She drove away quickly, scattering the crowd, and turned the jeep expertly into the narrow side street.

"Where are we going?" he said.

"To the hotel for your things. Afterwards I'll take you out to the villa. Oliver would want me to."

She turned into the square and braked to a halt in front of the hotel. As she started to get out, Lomax laid a hand on her arm. "Not you, only me." He climbed down and walked round to the other side. "I could do with some time to think this thing out."

She looked down at him gravely. "Just as you like."

"Are you going to keep Yanni with you?"

She nodded. "I think it would be better."

He smiled and ran his fingers through the boy's tousled hair. "We'll find you another dog, Yanni."

He moved between the tables and just as he reached the door she called to him. When he turned he saw that she was unfastening a chain that hung around her neck.

She threw it to him, liquid gold in the sun, and he caught it, closing his hand over it at once, knowing what it was.

"I give you back your courage," she said, and drove away very quickly.

He went into the cool darkness, aware of Anna's frightened face peering at him from the kitchen doorway and the stairs seemed to stretch into eternity.

When he reached his room, he closed the door very carefully and stood with his back against it staring at his clenched right hand with the two ends of gold chain hanging down. After a while, he opened it gently and looked at the small bronze coin that bore the face of Achilles.

A long time ago, he thought. A hell of a long time ago. He lit a cigarette and went and lay on his back on the bed and stared blindly into the past.

Book Two

The Nightcomer

5

Cover of Darkness

It was the throb of the diesels that brought Lomax awake
with a start. He lay there for a moment on the bunk,
staring up at the steel bulkhead, a slight frown on his
face as he tried to remember where he was.

After a while, something clicked and he pushed himself
up on one elbow. Alexias was sprawled in a canvas chair
in the far corner watching him.

The Greek removed the cigarette that smouldered between his lips and grinned. "You talk in your sleep, my
friend. Did you know that?"

"That's all I needed," Lomax said. "Have you got one
of those to spare?"

The Greek nodded and rose to his feet. He was a big,
dangerous looking man badly in need of a shave and his
massive shoulders swelled under the blue reefer jacket.

"I think that maybe you've been playing this game too
long," he said as he gave Lomax a cigarette and struck
a match.

"Haven't we all?"

Before the Greek could reply, the curtain was pulled
back and Sergeant Boyd appeared with two cups of
coffee. He gave one to Alexias and the other to Lomax
who took a sip and grimaced. "Everything tastes of submarine. I don't know how they put up with it."

Boyd was a big, dependable northerner with the ribbon
of the Military Medal sewn neatly into place above his
left breast pocket beneath the SAS wings.

"We've just surfaced," he said. "Commander Swanson

asked me to tell you to be ready to go in fifteen minutes."

"Is all the gear ready?"

Boyd nodded. "I had to occupy myself somehow. Couldn't sleep. Never can in these things."

"How do you feel?" Lomax asked.

"About the job?" Boyd shrugged. "The same as usual. Why?"

Lomax shook his head. "No special reason. We seem to have been doing this sort of thing rather frequently lately, that's all. We can't last for ever, you know."

"Neither can the war," Boyd told him. "In any case, it's fifty-fifty every time. Even I know that much mathematics."

"I don't know," Lomax said. "This one's different. In Crete, a man could run a long way in those mountains, but Kyros is a small island."

"We've been on small islands before," Boyd told him. "Besides, we've got Alexias here to show us around. We'll be all right."

Alexias grinned and his teeth looked very white against the dark stubble of his beard. "Sure, everything's going to be fine. You've got nothing to worry about."

"Who said I was worried?" Lomax swung his legs to the floor. "You two get the stuff together. I'll see you up top in five minutes."

After they had gone, he sat there on the edge of the bunk finishing his coffee. It tasted foul, but then so did the cigarette.

He was tired, that was the trouble. Too damned tired and everything was beginning to blur a little at the edges. He definitely needed a rest after this one. A month in Alex should do it, but he'd been promised that for a year now. He pulled on his sheepskin coat, reached for his beret and moved outside.

He moved through into the control room and mounted the conning-tower ladder to the bridge. Above him, the round circle of the night was scattered with brilliant stars and he breathed the fresh salt air deep into his lungs and suddenly felt better.

Swanson was looking towards the shore, night glasses raised to his eyes. Lomax extinguished his cigarette and moved beside him. "How's it going?"

"So far without a hitch," Swanson said.

They were moving through a scattering of jagged rocks and tiny islands and Lomax whistled softly. "Looks pretty dicey to me."

"We didn't have a great deal of choice," Swanson told him. "After all, you did want to be on this side of the island and at least this gives us some sort of cover against their radar. They tell me the harbour here is usually crammed with E-boats. Care to take a look?"

Lomax took the night glasses and immediately the cliffs jumped out of the darkness at him, white surf pounding in across the rocks.

Swanson was speaking into the voice-pipe and when he turned his teeth gleamed in the darkness. "Not long now. How do you feel?"

"Fine," Lomax told him. "You don't need to worry about us."

"Of course you've done this sort of thing rather a lot, haven't you? I must say I like the look of your sergeant."

"We've been together two years now," Lomax said. "Crete, Rhodes, all over the Aegean. He knows more about explosives than any man I ever knew. Used to be a shotfirer in a Yorkshire pit before the war. They tried to defer him, but he wasn't having any of that."

"How does he handle the language problem?"

"He's picked up enough Greek and German to get by, but it doesn't really matter. I'm fluent in both languages."

"That's interesting," Swanson said. "What were you doing before this lot blew up?"

"University, journalism. A little writing." Lomax shrugged. "I hadn't really got started on anything properly."

"The war, the war, the bloody war," Swanson quoted. "I know what you mean. I was a third-year medic and look at me now."

They were close inshore and he glanced up at the single peak of the island, black against the night sky. "Don't the locals believe Achilles is buried on top of the mountain?"

Lomax nodded. "So they say. The Monastery of St. Anthony is up there too."

"You seem to know your way around."

"Not really. That's where Alexias comes in. He was born and raised here. We couldn't do this job without him."

"He's a rough looking customer," Swanson said. "Has he been with you long?"

Lomax shook his head. "He's been working with a group in Southern Crete. Intelligence brought him out specially for this particular show."

"How are you getting out when the job's done?"

"The Special Boat Service are handling that end. Using a Greek caicque and pretending to be fishermen. A bloke called Soames is in charge."

"I know him well," Swanson shuddered. "You'd be better off with the Jerries."

"We'll survive," Lomax said.

"I was talking to a chap in one of the bars at Shepheard's last week," Swanson said, "and he told me that Oliver Van Horn was still living here. That the Germans have left him alone. Is that true?"

"So I understand," Lomax said. "He came here just before the war because of his tuberculosis. I don't suppose he can do them much harm and allowing him to continue to live on the island makes for good publicity. Have you read any of his books?"

Swanson nodded. "One or two. Rather Maughamish with wonderful characterisation."

"I wish I had half his talent," Lomax said feelingly.

Swanson had been watching the shoreline carefully through the night glasses and now he leaned down and spoke briefly into the voice pipe.

The submarine started to slow and he turned to Lomax and said crisply, "This is as far as we go, I'm afraid. They're bringing your dinghy and gear out through the forward hatch. You'll find your sergeant and the Greek down there waiting for you."

"Thanks for the ride," Lomax said.

They shook hands briefly and he went over the side and descended the ladder to the circular hull. The dinghy was already in the water and as he arrived, Boyd dropped down into it followed by Alexias.

There was quite a swell running and the three ratings holding the lines cursed and one of them slipped and lost his footing on the slimy steel plates of the hull.

The Chief Petty Officer in charge handed the submachine guns and the radio pack to Boyd and then turned to Lomax. "I'd strap my pack on if I were you, sir. It's going to be a bit tricky going in through that surf."

"That's an understatement if ever I heard one," Boyd called softly.

Lomax slipped his arms through the straps of the heavy pack and buckled it securely.

"Ready to go, sir?" the CPO said.

"No time like the present, Chief."

He waited, judging the distance, and as the dinghy lifted on the swell, stepped into her and sat down at once. The ratings released the lines and immediately the tide pulled the dinghy away from the submarine and in towards the shore.

The wind was freshening, lifting the waves into whitecaps. As he reached for the paddle, the dinghy heeled and water poured over the gunn'l. He adjusted his weight and started to paddle.

Through the curtain of spray the cliffs loomed larger

and at their feet waves rolled in to dash upon jagged, dangerous looking rocks.

Boyd was cursing steadily as water slopped over the sides and Alexias plunged his paddle deep into the water, using his great strength to control their progress. And then they were lifted high on a great swell and Lomax saw the base of the cliffs no more than a hundred yards away.

For a moment they seemed to poise there and then they swept down between two great rocks. Strange, swirling currents twisted them in a circle and there was a hollow, slapping sound against the bottom of the dinghy.

The water broke into white, foaming spray that soared high into the air and then they slewed broadside into the surf and lifted high over a great slab of rock.

Lomax went over the stern into the boiling water and floundered to his knees, groping for the radio pack. As his fingers fastened over its straps, another wave sent him staggering.

He tried to stand up and Boyd plunged through the boiling surf, hands outstretched to help him. For a moment they clung together and then another great wave cascaded across the reef bowling them over.

Lomax instinctively released his grip on the radio pack and grabbed for Boyd. He held on desperately, the fingers of his free hands hooked into the gravel as the wave receded with a great sucking sound.

He forced himself to his feet, pulling Boyd up with him, and then Alexias appeared on the scene. Water boiled waist-high again, tugging at their limbs, and as it receded the three of them staggered over the final line of jagged rocks. A moment later they were safe on the white strip of beach at the base of the cliff.

Lomax slumped down, his back against a rock, and Boyd sat beside him. "You all right, sir?"

Lomax nodded. "It was pretty tricky there for a moment."

"I managed to hang on to the weapons," Boyd told him. "It was a damned good job we had the packs strapped on."

"I'm afraid the radio's gone," Lomax said.

Boyd's teeth gleamed in the darkness. "Never mind. At least it saves you from the temptation of using it when you shouldn't."

Alexias squatted beside them. "I managed to grab the dinghy." There was a hiss as he opened the valves and started to collapse it.

"Thanks for the strong arm," Lomax told him. "It was a lot rougher than I thought it was going to be."

Alexias looked across at the white surf pounding in over the jagged reef and shrugged. "On this side of the island the sea is like a woman. You never know what she's going to do next. As a boy, I've swum from this beach on hot summer nights when the water looked like black glass."

"We're here in one piece except for the radio and that's the main thing," Lomax said. "How far is it to your brother's farm?"

"About two miles and the going is easy."

"Then the sooner we get there the better." Lomax got to his feet. "According to Intelligence, there's an hourly patrol even on this side of the island."

They hastily covered the dinghy with sand and rocks and then Boyd distributed the sub-machine guns. They moved off at once, Alexias leading the way and Lomax bringing up the rear.

The sand was deep, and once he stumbled and cursed softly and then they were on a narrow path that mounted steeply through a ravine to the top of the cliffs.

Alexias held up a hand and moved forward cautiously and raised his head above the lip of the ravine. After a moment, he waved them on and they crossed a plateau of short, burnt grass and climbed a boulder-strewn hillside.

No word was spoken for at least half an hour and then they came over the shoulder of the mountain and saw a house standing in a grove of olive trees in a small valley below.

Alexias paused to get his bearings and then went down the hillside through the shadows, not bothering to follow the path which zig-zagged its way along the terraces of vines.

The house was in darkness and they crouched by the fence and Lomax checked his watch. It was barely nine o'clock and he frowned. "They must go to bed early."

Alexias shrugged. "They lead a hard life, these people."

"Maybe so," Lomax said. "But we're not taking any chances." He turned to Boyd. "You go round to the front and I'll cover Alexias from this side, just in case."

Boyd moved off into the darkness and they gave him a couple of minutes before moving. Lomax dropped to one knee beside a horse trough in front of the barn and Alexias continued across the yard and mounted the steps to the porch. He opened the door cautiously and went inside.

Somewhere a horse moved uneasily in its stall and a dog barked hollowly in the distance. A small wind kicked dust into his face and Lomax wiped it away with the back of his hand and narrowed his eyes, wondering what was happening in the house.

There was a slight, eerie creaking as the barn door swung open and someone said softly in Greek, "Put down your gun and raise your hands."

It was the voice of a woman who, considering the circumstances, seemed surprisingly calm. He propped his sub-machine gun against the horse trough and turned to face her.

The barrel of a shotgun prodded against his chest and he saw that she was only a young girl, her head barely reaching the level of his shoulder.

"What are you doing here?" she asked. "Who are you?"

He calmly pushed the barrel of the shotgun to one side. "There's no need for that. I'm a friend. A British officer. I'm looking for Nikoli Pavlo. Is he at home?"

She leaned forward, her face a white blur in the darkness. When she spoke, the tone of her voice had altered perceptibly. "No, he isn't here."

"I see," Lomax said. "May I ask who you are?"

"Katina Pavlo, his daughter."

There was a soft whistle from the porch and he picked up his sub-machine gun. "Let's go inside. I think you're in for a surprise."

She followed him across the yard and when they mounted the steps to the porch, Boyd was standing in the doorway. "There's no one at home," he said. "But there's a fire in the living room and the lamp's still warm." He broke off when he saw the girl. "Who's this?"

"The daughter of the house," Lomax told him. "She was hiding in the barn."

He brushed past Boyd and entered a stone-flagged kitchen with whitewashed walls. Another door led into the large living room which was furnished very simply. A log fire burned in an open hearth and a wooden ladder gave access to the loft through a trapdoor in one corner.

Alexias was in the act of lighting a lamp which stood on the table in the centre of the room. He replaced the glass chimney and turned. For a long moment he and the girl stood looking at each other and then she dropped the shotgun and ran straight into his arms.

He lifted her from the ground and swung her round in a circle. "Katina, my little Katina! How you've grown." He put her down and held her at arm's-length. "Where's your father?"

The young face was very white, the skin drawn too tightly over the prominent cheekbones, the eyes in shadow. She shook her head slightly as if unable to speak and the smile vanished from Pavlo's face.

"What is it, Katina? Tell me!"

When she spoke, her voice sounded hoarse and unnatural. "He's dead," she said. "They shot him in front of the town hall last week."

She started to cry, great dry sobs wracking her slender body, and Alexias pulled her close to him and stared blindly into space. After a while, he led her across the room to the kitchen, dragging his feet like an old man, and the door closed gently behind them.

6

A Willingness to Kill

When Alexias came back into the living room some twenty minutes later, Lomax and Boyd were sitting in front of a roaring fire stripped to the waist, their clothes steaming on an improvised line.

The Greek slumped down into a chair and took out a cigarette mechanically. He seemed to have aged ten years and his eyes were full of pain as he sat staring into the fire.

After a while, he sighed. "He was a good man, my brother. Too good to go the way he did."

Lomax gave him a light. "What happened?"

"They caught him trying to sabotage an E-boat in the harbour."

"On his own?" Boyd said in surprise.

Alexias nodded. "Kyros is a small island. It just wouldn't be possible for any organised resistance movement to survive here. That's why I went to Crete two years ago. Nikoli wanted to come as well, but one of us had to stay. There was the farm and Katina to think of, especially as her mother had just died."

"How is she?" Lomax said.

"Katina?" Alexias shrugged. "It was nothing—a thing of the moment only. She has great courage that one. She is making coffee and preparing a little supper."

"What's she going to do?" Boyd demanded. "She can't go on living here on her own. She's only a kid."

"She's been staying with my wife. I have a bar down by the harbour called The Little Ship. Katina has been coming out here each day with the horse and cart to look after things until they decide what to do. Apparently she was just leaving when she saw us coming down the hill through the vineyard."

"Does she know why we're here?"

Alexias shook his head. "Not at the moment. I'll tell her later. She could be very useful to us."

"How much do you think the fact of your brother's death will interfere with our plans?" Lomax asked.

"Very little," Alexias said. "But it means I'll have to make personal contact with various local people myself now. As soon as we've had supper, I'll go down into the town with Katina."

"That could be dangerous," Boyd said.

Alexias shook his head. "There isn't a curfew in force on Kyros and the cafés on the waterfront are usually full until well past midnight. The Germans can alter many things, but not our way of life."

At that moment, the kitchen door opened and Katina came in. She was carrying a tray which she set down on the table.

She turned, brushing back a lock of hair from her forehead with one hand. "I'm afraid there is only cheese made from goat's milk and olives, but the bread is fresh. My aunt baked it this morning before I left."

"It looks bloody marvellous to me, love," Joe Boyd said, and she blushed and quickly poured coffee into four mugs.

Lomax had been pulling on his shirt and sweater at the fire and when he turned, he found her standing just behind him holding a mug of coffee.

She smiled shyly. "I'm afraid there isn't any sugar."

Her face was heart-shaped with a pure white skin drawn too tightly over prominent cheekbones and there were dark sunken circles under her eyes. Her black hair was drawn back from her face and tied carelessly with a ribbon. She was perhaps sixteen or seventeen, but it was hard to be exact. She had that tired, too-old look that he had seen in the eyes of so many people recently.

He smiled and took a sip of his coffee. "It tastes good anyway. Aren't you having any?"

She shook her head. "My aunt will have supper waiting for me when I return."

She wore a faded print dress which had obviously been washed and mended many times and an ancient Norfolk jacket, two sizes too big for her and belted round her slender waist.

Lomax ran a finger lightly down one of the lapels. "Harris tweed. Nothing very Greek about that garment. Where did you pick it up?"

She flushed and he was at once sorry knowing that in some way his words had touched her pride. "New clothes are one thing it is impossible to obtain here," she said. "I was given this coat by a friend, Mr. Van Horn."

"You know Oliver Van Horn?" Lomax said in surprise.

"Everyone on Kyros knows Mr. Van Horn," she said. "He's a fine man."

"Is he still living in his villa out on the point?" Alexias demanded.

She nodded. "The Germans don't bother him. Since old Doctor Douplos died, Mr. Van Horn has taken his place. He's the only doctor available to the islanders."

"I'd forgotten he studied medicine as a young man," Lomax said. "Something else he has in common with Maugham. I'd give a lot to meet him."

"Who knows, perhaps you will." Alexias cut himself a large slice of cheese. "Katina, I've decided to go into town with you. Will it be safe?"

She nodded. "There should be plenty of people in the streets on a warm night like this."

Alexias turned to Lomax. "I'll be back first thing in the morning. I should have got things moving by then. You and Boyd can sleep here in the loft."

"I'll go and harness the mare," Katina interrupted. "If I'm not back soon Aunt Sarah will begin to worry."

The door closed behind her and Lomax pulled on his tunic and reached for the night glasses. "She's got a point there. I'll give her a hand and then have a look round."

Alexias poured himself another coffee and moved to the fire, steam rising from his sheepskin coat. "I'll be ready to leave in five minutes. Just give me time to dry out a little."

Boyd was still making inroads into the bread and cheese as Lomax went through the kitchen and moved out on to the porch. He crossed the yard to the barn and paused in the entrance.

An old oil lamp swung from a beam that seemed to be the mainstay of the building and in its light Katina Pavlo was harnessing the mare. A board creaked under his foot as he went forward and she turned at once, reaching for the shotgun that leaned against the end of the stall.

She relaxed visibly. "Oh, it's you, Captain Lomax."

"So your uncle told you my name," he said.

She nodded. "You are younger than I had imagined. Much younger."

He frowned slightly. "I'm afraid I don't understand."

"Even on Kyros we have heard of the Nightcomer," she explained. "And of the things you have done in Crete. Last month all they could talk about in the cafés was of how you had kidnapped the German general on Rhodes and smuggled him out of Egypt. Even the Germans find difficulty in keeping such things secret."

"Tales grow in the telling," he said. "Remember that."

She slipped the bridle over the mare's head and fastened the strap quickly. "Your Greek is very good—too good for an islander."

He grinned. "I spent five years in Athens as a boy. My father was an official at the British Embassy there."

"I see."

She started to lead the mare from her stall and Lomax moved forward quickly. "Can I help?"

She nodded. "The cart's over there in the corner. If you could bring it here."

It was a light, two-wheeled affair and he tilted it forward as she backed the mare between the long curving shafts. He strapped the harness expertly into place on one side and she did the same at the other.

When they had finished, she smiled across at him. "You've done that before."

He nodded. "My grandfather was a farmer. That's all I wanted to be when I was a boy."

"And now?"

He shrugged. "My talents seem to run to darker things. I don't think there will be much demand for the qualities I possess after the war."

"But what happens now doesn't count," she said. "Not for any of us. There is a saying we have—Time out of mind. That is what the war is—a dark dream that has no meaning when the morning comes."

There was a passionate sincerity in her voice and in the soft, diffused light of the lamp, the tiredness and pain were washed away from her face and she looked very young. For a moment he wanted to tell her that life was so often not what it should be, but what it was, but he didn't have the heart.

"Let's hope you're right," he said lamely.

She nodded confidently. "If I wasn't, life would be a mockery."

He paused to light a cigarette and then followed at the tail of the cart as she led the mare outside. The night air was warm and scented, the sky like a black velvet cushion scattered with diamonds.

They stood side-by-side, shoulders touching, and she sighed with pleasure. "On a night like this it's possible to forget even the war for a little while. Oh, there is so much

I could show you if things were different."

"If I were an English tourist straight off the Athens boat?" he chuckled. "Where should we begin?"

"That's easy," she said. "The Tomb of Achilles. We would visit it once by moonlight and again at dawn when there is mist on the mountain. Life could show you nothing more beautiful."

"If you were there, satisfaction would be guaranteed," he said gallantly, and turned and looked at the peak dark against the night sky. "The Monastery of St. Anthony is up there, isn't it?"

He could hear the swift intake of her breath and her body stiffened. She turned and peered up at him. "So that is why you're here?"

"I don't understand?" he said.

"Please, Captain Lomax. I'm not a fool. Everyone on the island knows that the Germans took over part of the monastery three months ago to use as a radar station."

He shook his head. "Not as a radar station, Katina. It's rather more important than that."

"I see," she said. "And you intend to destroy it? But the monks are still living there."

"If they weren't, we'd have bombed the place long ago," he said. "That's why the Germans force them to go on living there. Typical Nazi trick. They tried it on a big scale at Monte Cassino in Italy, but it didn't work. The place was blasted off the face of the earth."

"Then why hasn't the same thing been done here?" she demanded. "Since when have the lives of twenty or thirty old monks been important to either side in this war?"

"Because there's no need," he said, surprised at the bitterness in her voice. "Because my way is simpler and cheaper and with any kind of luck, no one should get hurt."

"Except possibly yourself. You forget that."

He grinned. "Something I learned to forget about a long time ago. It doesn't pay."

She was about to reply when he heard a sound faintly in the distance and laid a hand on her arm. "Just a minute."

They waited, and as the sound grew louder, Katina said, "It's the patrol."

"How many?" he demanded.

"Usually two, but sometimes one. They follow the cliff paths in a motor cycle and sidecar."

He raised the night glasses and as he focused them the noise of the engine grew louder and the motor cycle appeared on the rim of the valley and paused.

The sidecar was empty, but he could clearly see the steel-helmeted driver, strangely anonymous in his goggles as he looked down into the valley. A moment later, the engine roared into life again and the machine descended the track in a great cloud of dust.

"Do they usually call at the farm?" Lomax said.

She shook her head. "Occasionally they stop and ask for coffee, but not very often."

He took her arm and they turned and ran for the house. Alexias and Boyd met them at the kitchen door and the Greek was holding one of the sub-machine guns.

"Trouble?" he said.

Lomax nodded. "German patrol. One man on a motor cycle."

Joe Boyd pulled a gun from the soft leaather holster that hung beneath his left armpit under his shirt. It was a Mauser automatic with an SS bulbous silencer, a weapon much favoured by German counter-intelligence agents, souvenir of an earlier affair in Crete.

"Don't be a fool," Lomax said. "If we kill him they'll turn the island upside down. It would ruin everything.

"Captain Lomax is right," Katina said. "You must collect your things and go into the loft. When he arrives, I'll tell him I was just leaving."

There was no time to argue. They moved into the living room and Boyd mounted the ladder to the loft and opened the trapdoor. Lomax and Alexias quickly passed the packs and the rest of their equipment up to him and Katina put the remnants of the supper and the dirty crockery into a cupboard in the corner.

She extinguished the lamp, moved across to the kitchen door and turned to see if they were ready as the motor cycle roared into the yard outside. Lomax nodded briefly and went up the ladder to join Boyd and Alexias in the warm darkness.

Boyd lowered the trapdoor, jamming it open slightly with a piece of wood. Through the crack it was possible to see a little of the room below. A corner of the fire-place, most of the table and a chair beside it, but not the door.

They waited and Lomax thought about the girl, remembering her face as he had last seen it, very white, but strangely calm, and then they heard voices and the door opened. A moment later and the German moved into view.

He was almost as big a man as Alexias and the knee-length black leather jacket which covered his grey uniform was coated with white dust. He took off his helmet and gauntlets, dropping them on the table, and took out a cigarette. Without the helmet he looked younger and he ran a hand over his short blond hair and called to Katina in bad Greek.

Lomax couldn't hear what was said, but after a moment, Alexias leaned close and whispered, "She is making coffee. I can smell it."

The German got to his feet and disappeared from view, obviously going to lean in the kitchen doorway. A few moments later he returned to the table and sat down and Katina came into view carrying a tray.

As she reached for the coffee pot, the German grabbed her wrist and pulled her round. She tried to get away, making no sound, but he was too strong for her. He laughed once and Lomax closed his eyes and brushed sweat from his forehead.

When he opened them again, she was half across the table, the German sprawled on top of her, his hands moving over the young body.

Her face was bone-white and she seemed to look straight into Lomax's eyes. He felt his throat go dry and clenched his right hand and then she cried out sharply.

Before he could move, Alexias growled like an animal, sent the trapdoor back with a crash and scrambled through the opening. As he dropped, his right foot slipped between two rungs and he lost his balance and fell heavily to the floor.

The German turned in alarm. For a moment he stared down at Alexias in horrified surprise and then he pushed Katina away from him.

Lomax dropped through the opening and moved in fast. The German hastily unbuttoned the flap of his holster, but he was too late. As he drew his pistol, Lomax grabbed his wrist, pushing the weapon to one side, and raised his knee into the man's crotch.

The German grunted with pain, his head coming forward, and Lomax struck him sharply against the jaw with his right elbow, snapping the bone. The German screamed, his head going back as he fell against the table, and Lomax slashed him across the throat with the edge of his hand. The table went over with a crash and the German rolled on to his face.

Katina was already on her knees beside her uncle and Boyd was half-way down the ladder, his Mauser ready in his hand. He slipped it back into his holster and helped her raise Alexias into a sitting position.

The Greek's face was twisted with pain and there was a film of sweat on his forehead. "Mother of God, I think it's broken," he said.

Lomax crossed the room quickly and between them they got him to a chair. Alexias tentatively ran his hands down the leg and winced suddenly. "I was right. There's a break just below the knee. What a stinking mess."

Katina was near to tears. "I'm sorry," she said. "I did my best, but he wouldn't go away. He insisted that I must make him coffee."

Boyd was on his knees beside the German and now he stood up. "One thing's for sure—he'll never bother anyone again." He glanced at Lomax, face grim. "You never do things by halves, do you? A couple of hours from now and they'll be looking for this bloke all over the island."

"Then they must find him," Alexias put in.

Lomax turned, a frown on his face. "What do you mean?"

"For God's sake give me a cigarette," the Greek said. "It's simple enough. They patrol along the top of the cliffs in their motor cycles. He'll have to meet with a nasty accident, that's all."

"By God, he's right," Boyd said. "It's a way out."

Lomax nodded. "The only way, but there's still a snag. They probably won't find him till daybreak. That means this is going to be an unhealthy neighbourhood for the rest of the night. In any case, Alexias needs a doctor." He turned to the Greek. "How far is it to Van Horn's place?"

"Over the shoulder of the mountain, no more than an hour if you know the track."

Lomax frowned. "If you think we're leaving you here, you're crazy. When the Germans turn out, they're bound to search this place."

"I won't be here," Alexias said. "I'll be safe in town at The Little Ship. Help me on to the cart and I'll have myself there in half an hour."

"But what about me, uncle?" Katina said.

He managed a smile and patted her arm. "You must take them to Mr. Van Horn as soon as you can. With

63

luck he may be able to return with you to The Little Ship tonight."

"You seem to have it all worked out," Lomax said.

"The way he puts it, it's all we can do," Boyd told him.

Lomax nodded. "That's it then. Let's get him out to the cart before we do anything else. The sooner he's safe in town and off the road the better."

He and Boyd supported the Greek between them as they went outside and Katina brought the horse and cart across to the bottom of the steps. They helped him up on to the narrow seat and he supported his injured leg on one of the shafts.

Boyd went inside and came back with one of the submachine guns. Alexias slipped it under his seat and smiled down at them, teeth gleaming in the darkness.

"Don't worry. Everything's going to be fine. I feel it in my bones. This won't make any difference to the main plan. As soon as I get things moving, I'll be in touch."

He picked up the reins and moved away into the darkness and Lomax turned to Boyd. "We haven't got much time. Let's get our friend outside as quickly as possible."

Katina followed them and stood in the door watching as they pulled the German's gauntlets over his stiffening fingers and strapped on his helmet. As they brushed past her with the body, she turned her face away, but a few moments later as they eased the body into the sidecar, she came out on the porch.

"Who's going to drop him?" Boyd asked.

"I will," Lomax told him. "You get the kit down and be ready to move as soon as we get back."

Boyd nodded and ran up the steps into the house and Lomax turned to Katina. "I'm afraid I'll have to ask you to show me the nearest suitable spot."

She came down the steps without a word and he mounted the machine and waited for her to get on to the pillion. As soon as she was seated, he kicked the starter and let in the clutch.

They followed a well-defined path up out of the valley and then she pressed his shoulder and pointed and he swung the machine into a track that cut across the dark earth like a white line in the night.

The wind on his face carried the good fresh smell of the sea and he could taste the salt on his lips and then they came over a small rise and the dark line of the cliffs was no more than fifty yards below.

He cut the motor and turned as she dismounted. "Is this the place?"

She nodded. "The cliffs are a hundred feet high here. At their base there is an old jetty and a boathouse where my father kept his boat before the war for the fishing. Now the Germans have forbidden us to use it."

He pulled the body from the sidecar and laid it on the ground. Then he put the machine into neutral and let it roll towards the edge of the cliffs.

He hoisted the dead man on to his back and went down the slope. For a moment he stood at the edge, looking at the white line of surf breaking on the rocks below, and then he tossed the body down after the machine and went back to the girl.

She was standing at the top of the rise where he had left her and he was conscious that she was looking at him through the darkness.

"I'm sorry you had to get mixed up in this," he said awkwardly. "It's been a hell of a night by any standards."

She stood quite still without saying anything and he moved closer. "Are you all right?"

And then she started to cry and he put an arm round her gently, pulling her close. After a while, they started back through the darkness towards the farm.

7

Of Action and Passion

Oliver Van Horn's villa was perched on the extreme end of a narrow finger of rock that jutted out into the calm waters of a secluded bay on the other side of the headland from the town. It was a two-storeyed building with a flat roof and stood in a couple of acres of garden surrounded by a high wall.

They went down the hillside and crossed the white dusty strip of road and approached cautiously. The great, iron-bound gates stood open. They moved inside and Katina led the way along a narrow flagged path between olive trees.

The garden was a riot of color, the night air heavy with the scent of flowers. Palms lifted their heads above the wall and gently nodded in the cool breeze and a fountain splashed in a fish pool in a small clearing.

They could hear the low murmur of voices from somewhere near at hand and Katina moved forward quietly and crouched down.

They were on the edge of the circular driveway in front of the main entrance. A German command staff car was parked at the bottom of the steps and two NCOs in grey uniforms and forage caps lounged beside it smoking cigarettes.

A moment later, the front door opened and two men moved out into the lighted porch. Lomax recognised Van Horn at once from the many photos he had seen. Lean and wiry in a white linen suit, his clipped moustache and grizzled hair prematurely grey.

The other man was a German staff officer, a colonel of infantry and astonishingly young for such a rank with a mobile intelligent face.

He limped heavily as he went down the steps and climbed into the car and Van Horn stayed in the porch. He raised his hand as the car moved away, scattering gravel, and then went back inside.

As the door closed, Lomax turned to Katina. "Who was the German officer?"

"Colonel Steiner. He is in command here."

"They looked too bloody friendly for my liking," Boyd said.

She shook her head. "Mr. Van Horn depends on Steiner's goodwill for all his medical supplies. That's why he plays chess with him every week." She got to her feet. "I think it would be better if we went round to the rear of the house."

They followed another path round a corner and she paused in the bushes a few yards from a flight of shallow steps that led up to a covered terrace. A french window stood open to the night, curtains lifting in the wind, light spilling into the darkness.

Someone was playing the piano rather well, an old, pre-war Rodgers and Hart number, nostalgic and wistful, a hint of a summer that had gone and memories only now.

"Wait here!" Katina said.

She crossed the lawn, mounted the steps and went in through the french window. Lomax leaned against a tree, the sub-machine gun crooked in his arm, and waited.

The piano stopped. The silence which followed seemed to go on for ever and he could hear the waves breaking across the rocks on the beach below. Suddenly, the curtain was pulled back and Van Horn appeared.

He moved across the terrace, leaned over the balustrade and called softly, "Captain Lomax?"

Lomax stepped out of the bushes, Boyd at his heels, and crossed the lawn.

"My dear fellow, delighted to see you," Van Horn said as calmly as if he were greeting an old friend arriving for dinner. "Let's go inside."

The room was large and comfortably furnished, its low roof crossed by great beams. A grand piano stood against one wall and a fire of logs burned on a wide stone hearth.

There was no sign of Katina, but at that moment the far door opened and she came in followed by an old woman with brown wrinkled face and sharp black eyes. She was drying her hands on the white apron she wore over her dress and looked at them curiously.

Van Horn crossed the room, the three of them held a hurried conversation in Greek and then he returned.

"I've asked Maria, my housekeeper, to fix you up with a room and a meal. We'll have a chat when I get back."

"You're going into town?" Lomax said.

Van Horn nodded. "I shouldn't be long. The Germans took my car away long ago, of course, but I managed to get a couple of bicycles out of them for emergency calls."

"Is there anyone else here?"

"Only Maria. She's dumb, by the way, but she can understand everything you tell her." He turned to Katina. "We'd better get moving, my dear."

She was very pale and fatigue showed clearly on her face, but she looked up at Lomax and managed a wan smile. "I'll probably see you in the morning."

"Only when you've had at least twelve hours sleep," he told her.

"Don't worry, I'll see that she does." Van Horn slipped an arm about her shoulders and they left the room.

Later, after Maria had taken them upstairs and left them in the comfortable room with the twin beds at the end of the corridor, Lomax stood at the window looking out to sea and tiredness flooded through him.

Boyd had stripped to the waist and was washing his head and shoulders in cold water and Lomax followed suit. Afterwards, he felt better and they went downstairs and followed the aroma of coffee until they reached the kitchen where the old woman had prepared a meal of fried fish and eggs for them.

Later, they took their coffee and went back into the living room and sprawled in front of the fire smoking cigarettes.

"I think I can stand about as much of this as they've got to offer," Boyd said. "Another cigarette and it's me for bed. What about you?"

"I'll wait for Van Horn to show up," Lomax told him. "He'll probably have a message from Alexias about to-morrow."

Boyd got to his feet and moved across to the book-shelves that lined one side of the room. He examined one or two and chuckled. "All by the great man himself, bound in green leather and autographed in gold."

"Bring one over for me," Lomax said.

Boyd brought half a dozen and dropped them to the floor beside the chair. He was holding a slim pocket-book size volume in the same edition and there was an expression of real interest on his face.

"This one's called *The Survivor*. Seems to be mostly poems about the war."

Lomax nodded. "He was in the trenches during the last lot."

"I think I'll take it to bed with me," Boyd said. "Find if he knows what he's talking about. I'll see you later."

When he had gone, Lomax picked up a novel at random and leafed through it. It was one he had read before, but as always he was gripped by the narrative skill. It must have been an hour later when the curtains were pulled aside and Van Horn stepped through the french window.

He was carrying an old Gladstone bag, the leather scuffed and fraying, and he dropped it carelessly on the divan.

"Ah, there you are. What happened to your sergeant?"

"Gone to bed with a volume of your war poems. I hope you don't mind?"

"Not as long as I get it back. You know, Lomax, for some strange reason, most people seem to think writers ought to distribute their books free." He sighed. "My God, but it's a pull up that hill out of town. I'm not as young as I was."

His eyes were tired, the face lined with fatigue. He crossed to a cupboard in the corner, opened it and took down a bottle and two glasses. "The last of the gin."

"Don't waste it on me," Lomax said. "I'm only passing through to the main bar at Shepheard's, so to speak."

Van Horn grinned and slumped down into the opposite chair. "Nonsense, this is something of an occasion. Not often I get a little civilised company."

"Doesn't Colonel Steiner count?" Lomax asked.

Van Horn raised his eyebrows. "Good heavens no! That's strictly business. I let him beat me at chess once a week and then he feels morally bound to give me all the medical supplies I ask for."

"We saw him getting into his car as we arrived," Lomax said. "He looked surprisingly young to me."

"Twenty-seven," Van Horn said. "Badly wounded at Stalingrad and evacuated just before the Russians closed the circle. He's got the Knight's Cross besides all the usual things and they don't give *that* away, you know."

"He sounds formidable," Lomax said. "Did you have any difficulty when you went into town?"

Van Horn shook his head. "Alexias had only arrived at The Little Ship about twenty minutes before we did. They got him up to bed and I had a look at his leg."

"Is it bad?"

"Bad enough. I've set the bone, given him sulfa drugs.

He should be all right if he rests for a week or two. He certainly won't be able to play an active part in your operation."

"Is there any message?"

"Only that he hopes to arrange a meeting with various people tomorrow afternoon. Katina will be up to let us know when."

"So he's included you in?"

"I'm afraid so." He poured himself another gin. "Katina was telling me you're here to do something about the radar station they've set up in the main tower at the monastery."

"It isn't radar," Lomax told him. "It's a little gadget that selects a target electronically. All their planes or E-boats have to do is follow the beam and they can't go wrong. They've been doing a lot of damage to our shipping lately."

"But is it all that important? I thought they were losing the war anyway, particularly since the landings in Normandy last month."

"There's a faint chance of an invasion of Crete in the near future in which case this installation on Kyros could be a nuisance, but the Aegean is only a sideshow now, if that's what you mean. I don't think anything that happens here can affect the ultimate course of the war one iota." He grinned wryly and swallowed some of his gin. "On the other hand, they've got to keep us busy, haven't they?"

"Now I find that rather an interesting observation," Van Horn said. "What were you doing before the war?"

"University, a little journalism," Lomax shrugged. "Nothing very much."

"And then the war came along with an easy answer to all your problems." He nodded at the medal ribbons on Lomax's tunic. "It would appear you've had an active time of it since."

"I suppose you could say that."

"Have you enjoyed it?"

Lomax grinned reluctantly. "In my own twisted way."

"The willingness to kill. Very important in a soldier." Van Horn sighed. "Funny how the same word can mean something different. For me, war was the trenches. Mud and filth, brutality and death on an incredible scale. A whole generation wiped out. At times I feel like an anachronism."

"And for me?"

"A landing under cover of darkness, action by night, a chase through the mountains." Van Horn shrugged. "A week from now you'll be sitting in the main bar at Shepheard's having a drink to celebrate another bar to your MC. I strongly suspect that the day the war finishes, you won't know what to do with yourself."

"One slight point you've omitted to mention," Lomax said. "All Special Service officers are automatically shot when captured. That's a direct order from the German High Command and it's been in force for two years now. It adds a certain element of risk."

"And so it should," Van Horn said. "Life is action and passion: therefore it is required of a man that he should share the passion and action of his times at peril of being judged not to have lived." He grinned suddenly and sat back in his chair. "There I go getting emotional again. It's the writer in me taking control. In any case, Oliver Wendell Holmes said it first."

"I was hoping to be a writer myself one day," Lomax told him. "That's why I was so keen to meet you."

"Of arms and the man I sing, eh?" Van Horn got to his feet. "You should get something out of the war then, if only a book. Let's have a last cigarette on the north terrace. I think you'll approve."

He led the way through the hall and along a cool whitewashed corridor. The room they entered was in darkness, but Lomax could see that it was circular with glass walls. Van Horn opened a sliding door and they stepped outside.

Lomax sucked in his breath sharply. The terrace was cantilevered and the immediate sensation was that they were floating in space. The darkness was perfumed with the scent of flowers and the great bowl of the night dipped to meet the sea, stars glittering into infinity.

Two hundred feet below, waves slopped lazily over the rocks in a white cream at the base of the cliffs. "I've never seen anything like it," Lomax breathed. "In a setting like this how could a man help but write?"

"That's what I used to think," Van Horn said. "And then came the war. Later, old Doctor Douplos passed on and I remembered that in a moment of youthful abberation, I'd actually trained as a doctor. Since then I don't seem to have had the time."

"Perhaps when the war's over."

"Who knows?" Van Horn shook his head. "When I stand here and think of the stupidity of man I wonder whether I'll ever want to write about him again. At times like that I have to go and take a look at my collection to reassure myself that life is still worth living."

"Your collection?" Lomax said.

Van Horn nodded. "I'll show you if you like."

He led the way back inside, closed the sliding door and crossed the room.

Lomax heard the click of a switch, but was totally unprepared for what followed. On every side, a row of glass showcases, each with its own illumination, sprang into view to float in darkness.

But it was their contents which drew an involuntary gasp of admiration from him. They contained the most superb collection of Grecian pottery he had ever seen.

Van Horn moved beside him, face disembodied in the light of the nearest showcase. "There's more than a hundred thousand pounds' worth here—just by commercial standards. In actual fact, some of this stuff is priceless."

His voice had taken on an added warmth and Lomax moved from case to case, examining the contents with interest. He finally halted before a superb Grecian wine amphora at least three feet high, the red and black colours in the design still vivid after two thousand years.

"That can't be genuine and still in one piece."

"It came from a tomb under the Temple of Apollo on Rhodes. The Greek government were excavating there just before the war." Van Horn grinned. "By rights it should be in Athens, but I came to an arrangement with the rather underpaid young government official who found it."

"It's one of the most beautiful things I've ever seen," Lomax said.

"The handiwork of man, that's what still gives me hope, though what to make of some of the stuff they were churning out during the twenties and thirties and calling art, I'll never know."

"On the other hand, some of these are hardly representational." Lomax indicated a case containing several early Cretan figurines, mostly crude images of the Earth Mother.

Van Horn chuckled. "You've got a point there."

He put out the light and they went back along the corridor to the hall. As they went upstairs, he said, "I know we haven't got much time, but with luck we should be able to have a long talk in the morning. I expect you could use some sleep now."

He said good-night and Lomax went along to his own room and lay on the bed, listening to Boyd's easy breathing, and went over the night's events.

He kept thinking about Katina Pavlo, remembering how pale and tired she'd looked when he had last seen her. His last conscious thought was of her face glowing in the darkness and the strange thing was that she was smiling at him.

8

"The Little Ship"

It was just after noon on the following day when Katina turned the cart into the main square of Kyros and the Nazi flag hung like a limp rag in the great heat.

Lomax sat beside her, his back against the load of firewood they carried, one foot on a shaft, the other swinging idly.

In the old reefer jacket, broken boots and shabby tweed cap she had brought him, he looked like a typical peasant from one of the mountain farms.

Katina had a scarf round her head peasant-fashion and wore a faded print dress with no sleeves that made her arms look very thin. She'd hardly spoken since leaving Van Horn's villa, but her eyes were clear and there was a freshness to her face that indicated that she had slept well.

She reined in the mare as a squad of soldiers in field grey cut across their path and Lomax eyed them with professional interest.

"Old men and boys," he said as they started forward again. "They've been draining Greece and the islands of their best troops for months now. At least it proves who's winning the war."

As they turned on to the waterfront, he leaned forward to get a view of the harbour. The brightly painted caicques were all drawn up on the strip of beach and fishermen sat in the shade of the stone wall and mended their nets.

An E-boat moved out to sea, churning the water at its

stern into a white froth, sending waves rippling across the surface of the harbour.

Several more were moored to the pier, their crews busy on deck, stripped to the waist in the hot sun, cleaning and polishing.

"Are there always as many E-boats in the harbour?" Lomax said.

She nodded. "There are as many as you see here out on patrol."

She turned the mare into a narrow side street on the corner of which stood The Little Ship and Lomax dropped to the ground and went and opened the double gates that gave access to the yard at the rear of the building.

He pulled a small military pack from under the firewood and they went inside and moved along the whitewashed corridor. He could hear the murmur of voices, a glass clinked and someone started to play a gay tune on a *bouzouki.* There was a bead curtain at the end of the corridor beside a flight of stairs and Katina motioned him to stay and went through.

He peered through the curtain into the bar. It was a cool, pleasant room with whitewashed walls and a vaulted roof like a wine cellar. It was crowded with fishermen. There didn't seem to be a single German soldier in the place.

The curtain parted and Katina stepped through followed by a round-faced, kindly looking woman in her late thirties with bright blue eyes.

"This is Aunt Sarah," she said. "The others are already here and waiting in my uncle's room. Mr. Van Horn arrived ten minutes ago."

Mrs. Pavlo smiled and led the way upstairs.

"She seems to be taking all this with remarkable calm," Lomax whispered.

Katina smiled. "She has been married to my uncle for twenty years. She says anything can happen and usually does. She loves him very much."

Mrs. Pavlo opened a door at the head of the stairs and led the way in. The room was hazy with tobacco smoke. Alexias was propped up in a great bed, his pipe in his mouth. There were several other people in the room, but the only one Lomax knew was Van Horn who sat beside the bed, smoking a cigarette in a silver holder.

"Ah, Lomax, my good friend. We've been waiting for you." Alexias grinned. "Here he is, everybody. The Nightcomer in the flesh."

There was a sudden silence as they all turned to look at Lomax curiously and he moved quickly from person to person as Alexias introduced them.

The parish priest, Father John Mikali, was first by convention. A dignified old man with a white beard and sombre in his dark robes, he showed no emotion at all and Lomax sensed a coldness in his manner.

A tall, bearded man named John Paros came next. He looked like the captain of a fishing boat and turned out to be the local electrician. Sitting beside him in the corner was Alexias's brother-in-law, Nikoli Aleko. Small and wiry with blazing blue eyes, he helped his sister run The Little Ship.

George Samos and Yanni Demos came forward last of all. Both in their early twenties with crisply curling hair and tanned faces, they might have been brothers. They shook hands, undisguised admiration on their faces.

"Have you brought what I asked for?" Alexias demanded.

Lomax dropped the small military pack on the end of the bed. "It's all there."

"Good, then we can get down to business."

"A moment, Alexias," Father John interrupted. "There is a question I should like to put to Captain Lomax before we go any further."

There was a sudden tenseness in the air and Lomax sensed that whatever matter the old priest intended to raise had already been discussed before his arrival.

"Your mission here, Captain Lomax," he said. "Just how important is it?"

Lomax knew that Van Horn was gazing at him steadily, but he never faltered. "Very important," he said calmly.

"But how can this be?" Father John said gently. "The Germans are losing the war, the whole world knows it to be only a matter of time. Can the destruction of a radar station or whatever else it may be on one tiny island in the Aegean have any real effect on the ultimate end?"

"If that argument were pursued to its logical end in every theatre of the war, the ending might be different," Lomax pointed out. "May I ask why you've raised this issue?"

"As parish priest I have the welfare of my people to consider above all things," Father John said. "Forgive me for stating the obvious, but after the completion of your mission, you will leave Kyros. We, on the other hand, must remain to face the wrath of the Germans."

"I know that, Father," Lomax said.

"Are you also aware that when the Germans discover the identity of anyone guilty of an act of aggression, they now arrest his immediate family also and send them to the concentration camp at Fonchi on the mainland? In Katina's case, Colonel Steiner made an exception only because Mr. Van Horn and I made personal pleas for clemency on the grounds of her extreme youth. Now the child is to be involved in something infinitely worse."

"You should come to Crete, Father," Alexias growled. "I've seen entire villages wiped out as reprisals for our success. Men and women hanging from the olive trees like ripe fruit. It only made the people hate the harder."

"We've put up with the Germans for three years, Father," John Paros said quietly. "Kyros is a small island. Up till now there hasn't been much we could do. This is probably our only chance to make a contribution."

Katina moved forward and dropped to one knee beside

the old priest's chair. "Don't worry about me. My father gave his life. How can I offer less?"

Father John gently touched her head, then he gazed round the room and nodded. "So be it. It becomes evident that I am on my own in this matter."

There was an audible sigh of relief from everyone and Nikoli Aleko passed Lomax a glass of red wine. "Luck to our venture," he said with a grin.

Lomax toasted him and Alexias said, "This is the way things go. Tomorrow is the feast of St. Anthony. As usual the whole island will make it a gala day. Every soldier who isn't actually on duty will be in town enjoying himself."

"What about the monks?"

"Usually most of them take part in the religious procession. Father John will make sure they all do this year. They'll leave the monastery at three in the afternoon and would normally be due back by six at the outside."

"What's the situation at the monastery?"

"One sentry at the main entrance in a box. During the day the gates are left open, but there's a swing bar. The tower is on the other side of a tiny square. The guard room is on the ground floor."

"What about communication with the town?"

"Telephone, but Paros here will cut the wires at the right time. He knows what to do. He's been working for them. There's also a short-range transmitter in the installation section of the tower. Nothing we can do about that."

"How many on duty?"

"Three in the guardroom, four on the installation itself. That's on the fifth floor, by the way. It can only be reached by a circular stone staircase."

"That sounds straightforward enough," Lomax said. "How do we get in?"

"That's where George and Yanni come in." Alexias nodded towards the two young men. "They have a shepherd's hut near the top of the mountain. Katina will take you up there sometime tonight."

"Then what happens?"

"There's a ration truck from the town to the monastery every afternoon at three-thirty. You know how methodical the Germans are. George and Yanni will block the road with sheep for a few minutes. It's up to you to handle the driver."

"And we drive the truck straight into the monastery?" Lomax said.

Alexias nodded. "George and Yanni have volunteered to go in with you. They can hide in the back. You or Boyd can wear the driver's uniform."

"That should place us at the monastery at about three forty-five," Lomax said. "How long will it take them to reach us from town after they hear the explosion?"

"Quite some time, because they'll be on foot." Alexias grinned. "You crossed a bridge over a deep ravine just outside town when you came in from Mr. Van Horn's villa. Tonight, Nikoli will use the explosive I asked you to bring, to mine it. The moment he hears the explosion at the monastery, he blows the bridge."

"And that cuts the only road on this side of the mountain," Lomax said. "The Germans won't be able to use their vehicles."

"I thought you'd like the idea." Alexias held out his glass for his wife to re-fill. "Compared to some of the jobs we've pulled on Crete, this will be easy."

"Except for the fact that the boat that's taking us off won't put in to the bay till nine o'clock," Lomax said. "That gives us roughly five hours on the run with Steiner turning the island upside down."

"When we took the general on Rhodes they chased us through the island for four days and still they couldn't catch us," Alexias reminded him.

"There was room to swing in Rhodes," Lomax said. "Still, we'll see how it goes."

"On the whole you agree to the plan, then?"

Lomax walked to the window and looked out over the harbour, a slight frown on his face. After a moment, he turned.

"Except for one thing. George and Yanni don't go in with us. They clear off as soon as they've stopped the truck."

Alexias frowned in bewilderment. "I don't understand."

"It's quite simple. Boyd and I can manage on our own once we get hold of the truck. In any case, we're going to go in in uniform. No peasant outfits this time."

"You must be mad!" Alexias said incredulously.

"I'm inclined to agree with you." Lomax helped himself to some more wine. "But it does leave a faint chance that Steiner might believe we pulled it off without any local help." He turned to the priest. "Best I can do, Father."

"I am grateful, Captain Lomax," Father John said. "You are a brave man."

"Or a fool," said Van Horn.

"I'll drink to that," Lomax said.

He half-turned, raising his glass, feeling suddenly reckless, and was aware that Katina was staring at him, eyes shining. For the first time since they had met, there was colour in her cheeks.

9

Temple of the Night

It was a quiet night, the only sound a dog barking in the depths of the valley from one of the hillside farms. The night sky was incredibly beautiful with stars strung away to the horizon where the mountain lifted uneasily to meet them.

Lomax looked at it all for several minutes and wondered why everything wasn't as simple and uncomplicated as a summer night. You only had to stand and look at it and it cost you nothing except a little time and gave so much.

Katina turned to wait for him and he moved on and a few minutes later they came over an edge of rock and the ruins of the temple lay before them in the centre of the plateau, bare and wind-swept, crumbling with the years.

The yellow sickle of the new moon touched the scene with a faint luminosity and the dark shadows of the half ruined pillars fell across the mosaic floor like iron bars.

"It's over here," Katina said.

He followed, boots clinking on loose stones, and they paused in front of a large, square tomb in chipped marble. It stood about six feet high and a half-obliterated frieze had been carved on each face.

"So this is the Tomb of Achilles," Lomax said.

"So they say." She turned and looked down towards the valley and the sea beyond. "What an incredible thing that on a night to thank God for, men should be occupied with thoughts of death and violence."

He dropped to one knee, cupping his hands to light a cigarette. When he looked up, she had moved to the far edge of the plateau.

She turned to come back and for a moment fear touched him. The moon was directly behind her and her image blurred at the edges. She looked unreal and ethereal and utterly transitory as if she might fly away at any moment. As soon as she moved, the spell was broken.

She sat on a stone, her back against the tomb, and he crouched beside her. "You'll have to be going soon, it's past midnight."

She nodded and leaned forward curiously. His shirt was open at the neck and in the moonlight the coin that he wore on the end of a gold chain was clearly visible.

"A religious medal?" she said.

He shook his head. "An old bronze coin with the head of Achilles on it."

She nodded as if suddenly understanding. "A good luck charm?"

"Something like that. I got it from an old fortune-teller in a back street in Alexandria just before I went on my first operation. She told me I'd meet great danger, but always with courage as long as I wore the coin."

"And you believed her?"

He grinned. "Not really. If I remember rightly, even Achilles was vulnerable when it came to the final show-down."

She hesitated and then said slowly, "When you killed the soldier at the farm last night, there was a coldness in you that frightened me. My Uncle Alexias kills because he hates the Germans. Why do you kill?"

"God knows, I certainly don't hate them." He shrugged. "Men like Boyd and myself have a talent for it, it's as simple as that. We do it because it has to be done."

"I see." There was another silence before she said, "Do you think you'll be successful tomorrow?"

"One can never tell. Something unexpected always

seems to happen, something not planned for. I think the real trouble will be in surviving until the boat picks us up."

"What do you intend to do?"

"I'm not too sure. We'll have to play it as it comes. We'll probably make for your farm and hole up somewhere near the bay where we landed. It's dark at seven-thirty. That should help a lot."

"Two years ago my father tried to grow tobacco," she said. "He dug a curing room out of the ground under the stables. The entrance is a trapdoor in the end stall and it's usually covered with straw."

"I suppose they'd find it soon enough if they made a thorough search of the place," he said. "But thanks for the idea." He got to his feet. "And now I think you should be moving."

They went down the hillside together to the little hollow in which the shepherd's hut stood. George Samos sat against a boulder keeping watch, a shotgun across his knees, a large black dog curled beside him for warmth.

He raised a hand in greeting and Lomax and Katina moved to the edge of the hollow and looked down into the valley.

Strange, but he was desperately conscious that there were things he wanted to say, but they wouldn't come to mind and then this strange, secret girl turned and smiled as if she was aware of the turmoil in his mind.

"You will be successful tomorrow, Hugh Lomax."

Their hands touched and then she turned and started down the hillside. For a little while he watched and then she dropped into the shadows of the ravine and was lost to him.

The hut was low roofed and built of great blocks of stone. Boyd squatted on a blanket beside the fire and fitted together a long-barrelled Winchester sporting rifle.

He glanced up as Lomax ducked through the entrance. "Has the kid gone?" Lomax nodded and Boyd continued, "They certainly breed them with guts in these islands."

He screwed the telescopic sight into position, raised the rifle to his shoulder and the hammer fell on an empty chamber.

"When we move out tomorrow afternoon you can leave that behind for a start," Lomax told him. "It only gets in the way at close quarters."

Boyd ran a hand lovingly over the stock. "Maybe you're right, but it's a lovely weapon all the same."

He loaded it carefully, laid it on the blanket beside him and then unbuttoned his tunic pocket and took out a slim, leather-bound volume.

As he opened it, leaning to the fire for light, Lomax said curiously, "What have you got there?"

"Van Horn's book of war poems." Boyd sighed. "I never was much of a one for this sort of thing, but I've got to give it to him. He certainly hits the mark."

"There's hope for you yet, then," Lomax said with a grin as Yanni poured coffee into battered tin mugs and handed them round.

Later, wrapped in a blanket, he lay in the corner and stared at the dying embers of the fire, wondering what he was doing here on top of a mountain on a tiny island in the Aegean.

But there was no answer, or none that would satisfy, and he turned his face to the wall and drifted into an uneasy sleep.

10

Fire on the Mountain

Lying there in the hollow between the rocks, the sun warm on his back, Lomax had been aware of the truck's approach for several minutes in spite of the bleating of the sheep as they moved reluctantly across the hillside.

He got to his feet and leaned across a boulder beside Boyd as the truck appeared around the shoulder of the mountain in the valley below. A few moments later it disappeared from view again behind a great outcrop of rock.

He moved out of the hollow and waved to George and Yanni who immediately started to drive their flock down the slope, pelting those at the rear vigorously with stones.

Lomax and Boyd went down the hill on the run, heels digging into the crumbling earth, and dropped into the ditch. Sheep milled around them, crying piteously, and George and Yanni wielded their long staffs, driving the bewildered animals up the steep bank until they blocked the narrow road.

Lomax could hear the truck start to slow and he nodded to Boyd and they crouched under an overhang where the dry soil had started to erode and then the truck had passed them and braked to a halt.

The driver leaned out of his cab and called angrily to George who stood a few yards away looking convincingly helpless as sheep milled around him.

The driver leaned further out of the window and shouted again. At that moment, Yanni came round the back of the truck and moved forward quickly. His long staff rose and fell across the unprotected neck with the force of a headsman's axe. The German made no sound and when the young shepherd reached up and opened the door, his lifeless body tumbled to the ground.

Lomax and Boyd were already scrambling out of the ditch and running towards the truck. Boyd stuffed his beret into a pocket of his camouflaged battle smock and pulled on the driver's grey forage cap. It was a size too small, but tilted down across the forehead was convincing enough to pass at a distance.

He scrambled behind the wheel and Lomax turned to Yanni who was on his knees going through the dead man's pockets. "Shove him into the ditch and get to hell out of here. You haven't got long, remember."

George Samos was already driving the sheep from the road and Boyd took the truck forward as Lomax climbed up into the cab from the other side. Within a few moments they were clear of the sheep and the noise fell away behind them as they turned another shoulder of the mountain and moved through a deep ravine.

As Lomax took Boyd's Mauser from one of his pockets and checked the silencer and the clip, they moved out of the ravine and the monastery came into view.

It was perched spectacularly on the edge of a small plateau which jutted from the side of the mountain like a shelf. Behind it, a wall of rock at least five hundred feet high blocked any other access.

Lomax crouched on the floor of the cab, his head and shoulders under Boyd's legs, the Mauser ready in his right hand.

Boyd kept the truck moving at a relatively fast speed. As he started to slow he said, "That's a bit of luck. He's raising the swing bar already."

"We'll still have to take care of him."

Boyd nodded. "Right, here we go."

He braked to a halt, keeping the engine ticking over, and opened the door. The sentry called out something which Lomax couldn't catch and came round the side of the door.

He was a small, undersized man in his forties and wore a pair of ugly steel military spectacles. His rifle was slung carelessly over one shoulder and there was a smile on his face.

Lomax gave him no chance. He grabbed him by the front of his tunic, pulled him forward and shot him between the eyes. He scrambled back, hauling the body up into the cab, and Boyd slammed the door and took the truck through the gates.

The slight, foolish smile was still frozen into place on the dead man's face, but blood poured from his nostrils and mouth. Lomax shoved him to one side as Boyd turned the truck in a half-circle and braked sharply at the entrance to the tower.

Lomax opened the door, jumped down to the steps and moved inside quickly, sub-machine gun ready It was cool and dark and very quiet. The first steps of the spiral staircase were only a few feet away, the door to the guardroom beside them. When someone inside laughed, it sounded remote and somehow unreal.

Lomax moved to the door, Boyd at his shoulder He wiped sweat from his brow with the back of a hand and nodded. Boyd opened the door quietly and they moved inside.

Two of the guards sat at a table playing cards in their shirtsleeves while the other lay on one of the narrow iron cots reading a magazine. One of the card-players cursed and threw down his cards. The other one started to laugh, his hand reaching out for the coins in the centre of the table, and then he saw Lomax and Boyd

"On your feet," Lomax said in German. "Do as you're told and live."

They stood up slowly, hands clasped behind their necks. The two card-players were little more than boys, but the one who had been reading the magazine was older with a hard, cold look to him and shrapnel scars down the side of his face.

He stared at them unwinkingly and Lomax said to Boyd, "Right, upstairs quick. I'll see to these three."

Boyd moved out and Lomax said, "Take off your belts and turn round."

One of the boys started to tremble and the man with the scarred face said, "Don't worry, son. They won't get very far."

"Shut your mouth and do as you're told," Lomax said. "If we could have afforded the noise, you'd be dead."

There was the sound of gunfire on the stairs. Instinctively, he glanced towards the door and the man with the scarred face kicked a chair at him and jumped for the arms rack on the wall.

Lomax turned, firing from the hip in a wide arc that drove the man against the wall and continued to cut down the two boys who still stood by the table, bewildered and uncertain. One of them screamed in his agony, heels drumming against the floor. Lomax finished him with another quick burst and turned and ran out into the hall.

As he reached the foot of the stairs, Boyd came round the corner. There was blood on his face where a piece of stone had sliced his cheek.

"Turned the corner and met one of them coming down," he said. "Too bloody quick for me. Closed some kind of steel trapdoor where the stairs pass through the first floor."

"They'll have every soldier in town up here before we know it," Lomax said. "And Nikoli isn't supposed to blow the bridge until he hears this lot go. You'll have to lay your charges here."

Boyd didn't argue. He took off his pack and opened it. The plastic explosive he was using was already made up into charges and Lomax helped him to fuse them quickly. Boyd placed them round the walls at spaced intervals. As he started to wire them up, an explosion sounded in the distance.

They looked at each other for a brief moment and then Boyd continued with his task, face calm. Something had obviously made Nikoli Aleko move ahead of time. Probably a vehicle had tried to cross the bridge and he had realised that something must have gone wrong.

"Is there enough?" Lomax demanded.

Boyd shrugged. "Depends how good the foundations are. In this climate, the mortar in these old buildings is usually pretty rotten."

He linked the wires to a small, battery-operated detonating box and nodded. "You get the truck moving. As soon as I hear the engine, I'll set this thing for thirty seconds."

Lomax moved outside quickly. The dead sentry still crouched on the floor of the cab, flies crawling over his face. Lomax dragged him out and clambered behind the wheel. The engine roared into life and as he moved into gear, Boyd ran out of the entrance and swung up beside him.

Lomax turned so tightly that the off-side wheels lifted. As they accelerated across the yard, someone fired a Schmeisser from one of the upper storeys, the bullets kicking fountains of dust into the air ten yards to the left and then they were through the gates.

The explosion, when it came, was tremendous and in the driving mirror Lomax saw a great cloud mushroom above the walls, the tower rising from its centre.

For a few moments it remained straight and true and then it seemed to lurch to one side. It started to fall in slow motion, gathering momentum as it disappeared into the dust and smoke.

Boyd had been leaning out of the window and he turned with a grin and wiped blood from his face with the back of his hand. "I don't mind telling you I was worried there for a moment or two."

"I still am," Lomax told him. "The sooner we're on the other side of the mountain, the better I'll like it."

He took the truck down through the ravine in a cloud of dust and braked sharply as they came out into the open. A German troop-carrier had just rounded the shoulder of the mountain a couple of hundred yards below and was moving towards them.

There were only seconds in which to act and he gave Boyd a shove towards the other door. "Get out of it," he shouted.

Boyd didn't argue. He jumped to the ground and Lomax took the truck forward in a burst of speed. A moment later, he opened the door and jumped.

The Germans seemed unaware of their danger until the last moment and then their driver swung the wheel of the troop carrier so sharply that the vehicle heeled over into the ditch as the empty truck rolled past. Fifty yards further on, it went over the edge of the road and disappeared from view as another troop-carrier came round the shoulder of the mountain.

As Lomax climbed out of the ditch and started across the road, a dozen soldiers ran towards him. He dropped to one knee and loosed off a long burst that sent them diving for cover and then continued across the road and began to scramble up the slope.

Behind him, the grey-clad figures fanned out as he worked his way up diagonally, keeping to the shelter of the boulders. He paused once and a bullet kicked up dirt uncomfortably close and he ducked and kept on moving.

They were close now, very close. He slipped, losing his footing, and slid back several paces on the steep slope and heard a cry of triumph behind him that was immediately followed by an explosion. As the echo died away, he heard not the sound of pursuit, but the cries of the wounded and dying.

As he got to his feet, Boyd appeared from behind a boulder a little further up the hill. His arm went back and a grenade curved through the air. Lomax ducked instinctively as it exploded and scrambled desperately up the last few feet and joined Boyd on a tiny shelf.

He turned, gasping for breath, and leaned against the boulder. Below them, the survivors of the first troop were still coming up the slope. At their backs, an exposed cliff lifted to the summit.

"Nikoli should have blown that bridge sooner," he said.

Boyd nodded. "This whole thing's beginning to stink."

On their left, the mountainside lifted steeply to the tiny hollow in which stood the shepherd's hut in which they had spent the night. The men from the other troop-carrier were already well up the slope, moving to cut off their retreat.

Lomax didn't hesitate. He moved out quickly and started across the slope, Boyd at his heels. Bullets thudded into the ground a few feet beneath them and he knew it could only be a matter of seconds until they found the range.

To keep going on the steep hillside was difficult enough, but Boyd paused and loosed off a wild burst to keep their heads down. The Germans didn't even bother to look for cover. They halted and started to fire in earnest and then, quite suddenly, one of them spun round and fell on his face and then another. Immediately, the whole group fanned out and dropped behind the nearest available cover.

Someone was firing at them from the hollow just below the rim of the mountain and Lomax slung his sub-machine gun round his neck and moved upwards, blood in his mouth, hands clawing at the loose stones.

He scrambled over the rim of the hollow, Boyd right behind him. Katina was lying behind a boulder, Boyd's Winchester sporting rifle to her shoulder. She fired two shots in rapid succession and moved beside him.

"What the hell are you doing here?" he demanded.

"I was worried," she said. "When I woke up this morning I had a bad feeling so I thought I'd come and wait for you at the hut. I found the rifle and the rest of your things and then everything started to happen at once."

Boyd was sitting with his back to a boulder. He'd lifted his battle smock and shirt and was in the act of pressing a field dressing against an ugly, puckered wound.

Lomax dropped to one knee beside him. "Is it bad?"

Boyd forced a grin. "Don't worry about me. I'll take my belt in another notch."

Katina peered over the edge of the plateau and drew back quickly. "They're very close."

"Right, we'd better get moving," he said.

He gave Boyd a hand and got him to his feet and they worked their way up the slope to the plateau and the Tomb of Achilles.

They crossed to the far rim and looked down the mountain to the other side of the island. Boyd's face was twisted with pain and sweat stood in great drops on his forehead. He turned despairingly to Lomax. "It's no go, I can't move fast enough. I'm just going to drag you down."

Lomax ignored him and turned to Katina. "I'll hold them here. Get him as far down the hillside as possible. In ten minutes, I'll make a run for it and try to lead them away. Get him down to the farm. I'll join you there after dark."

He took the Winchester from her and handed her Boyd's sub-machine gun. He didn't give either of them a chance to argue, but turned and ran back to the far edge of the plateau and dropped behind a boulder that gave him a clear view of the hut.

A soldier moved cautiously over the edge of the hollow. Through the telescopic sight, Lomax could see the eagle clearly on the man's tunic as he squeezed the trigger.

When he glanced back over his shoulder a moment later, he was alone.

11

No Hard Feelings, Captain Lomax

It started to rain as he went cautiously down the hillside towards the farm and fog rolled in from the sea pushed by a cold finger of wind. His mouth was dry and every bone in his body seemed to be aching.

He paused in the shelter of an olive tree and looked down into the hollow. The farm lay dark and still, rooted solidly into the ground, and he moved on down and ducked under the fence.

He paused at the horse trough, splashed water over his face with one hand and washed out his mouth. As he straightened, the barn door opened and Katina emerged.

"I was up in the loft watching for you," she said. "I'd begun to think you were never coming."

He sensed immediately that something was wrong and moved closer, peering down at her. "Where's Boyd?"

There was a moment's silence before she said slowly, "In the first stall. I couldn't get him any further."

Something in her voice told him what he would find, but he moved inside quickly, taking his electric torch from his pocket.

Boyd lay on his back in the straw, his sightless eyes partially retracted, the hands that had been folded neatly across his breast, already cold and stiff.

"He was all right until we reached the top of the hill," Katina said in a dead voice. "And then he had a hæmorrhage. I've never seen so much blood. It took me nearly an hour to get him down here."

She started to cry and he dropped the Winchester and

pulled her into his arms. Her slight body was racked with sobs and he held her close and gently stroked her hair.

After a while, she seemed to have control of herself and moved away. "I'm sorry. I'm behaving like a child. You should be getting down to the bay. You haven't got much time."

He was tired, more tired than he had been in four long years and nothing seemed to matter any longer. He took out a cigarette, lit it and blew out the smoke with a sigh and high up on the hillside the clear bell-like cry of a hound sounded on the night air.

She gripped his arm quickly and he said, "I thought I'd lost them in a water-course a mile back. It seems I was mistaken."

"There's still time," she said urgently.

He shook his head. "For you, Katina, but not for me. I'll try to lead them away. The moment the shooting starts slip out through the olive grove and work your way back over the mountain. I'll leave you the Winchester. It comes to pieces so you should be able to hide it easily."

"I won't leave you," she said.

He gripped her arms tightly. "Father John was right about me. Fighting and running, leaving other people to face the consequences. It's time I took some of the blame myself."

"But what purpose will it serve?" she said desperately.

"I don't know," he said. "It may help the people of Kyros, it may not. It'll be worth it if it only helps you."

She was crying again, her head against his chest. He tilted her chin, kissed her on the mouth once and then pushed her gently away. With a quick jerk he snapped the gold chain around his neck and dropped it and the coin into her hand. "I won't be needing this again."

He pulled Boyd into a sitting position, stooped and tilted him over one shoulder. The body was surprisingly light and when he moved outside, the cold rain stung his face, giving him a new energy.

The dogs were very close now and as he crossed the yard and moved along the track, they came over the crest of the hill above his head.

He broke into a shambling run and after a while turned off the track and moved across the barren hillside. He paused on top of a small rise, laid Boyd carefully down and turned, unslinging his machine gun.

They were coming down through the olive grove now and he loosed off a long burst. The dogs howled excitedly and he heard shouts and several shots were fired in reply.

He turned and started to run, but for some reason his legs refused to function properly and he tripped and fell heavily over a stone.

For a little while he lay there half-stunned and then he struggled to his feet. They had skirted the farm and were running along the track, men and dogs in full cry.

He raised the sub-machine gun and pressed the trigger, flame stabbing the night in a long, reverberating roll that emptied the gun.

He tossed the useless weapon to one side and turned to run as a Schmeisser stuttered in reply. It was as if he had been kicked sharply in the legs several times and he fell forward on to his face.

Everything was going away from him, but he was still conscious when a hand gripped him by the shoulder and turned him over and a torch was shone into his face. He could hear the excited voices of the soldiers and the snarling of the dogs as they were held back and the whole swelled into a meaningless roar and he plunged into darkness.

Slowly the blackness turned to grey and he was aware of somebody talking quietly near at hand. He opened his eyes and saw a light directly over his head like a baleful eye.

He was lying on a narrow operating table and when he moved slightly, the talking stopped and quick foot-steps sounded across a tiled floor. The man who leaned over him wore a neat white smock and was obviously a doctor.

"Just relax," he said. "You're going to be all right."

A male nurse moved beside him carrying a tray and the doctor filled a hypodermic and gave Lomax another injection. As he finished, a door swung open and Steiner came in and leaned over the operating table.

There was a faint smile on his face. "So, my dear Lomax. You are still with us?"

Lomax frowned, trying to push himself upright. "How did you know my name?"

The male nurse pressed a foot-pump, automatically raising one end of the table, bringing them face to face, and Steiner laughed. "I've got a file on you six inches thick in my office. Intelligence keep adding to it each month. I never thought we'd see you on Kyros, though. Excellent job you did on the monastery, by the way. Worth another bar to your MC I should imagine."

He took a cigarette from a slim gold case, put it in Lomax's mouth and lit it. "How do you feel?"

Lomax looked down and saw that his trousers had been cut open. Both legs were heavily bandaged. "As if I shouldn't be here."

"But you are," Steiner said. "Unfortunate, really. I'm supposed to have you shot. I presume you're aware of that?"

"I've had a good run," Lomax said.

"Of course a little co-operation might help me to change my mind," Steiner said. "The names of the people who helped you, for instance."

"I didn't need local assistance," Lomax said. "I had half a dozen good men with me."

"That's strange," Steiner said. "So far we've only accounted for you and the dead sergeant who was with you when you were picked up. How do you explain that?"

"The rest of my men must have made the rendezvous on time." Lomax glanced at his wrist-watch and tried to sound convincing. "We were due to be picked up by a submarine at eight o'clock on the other side of the island." He smiled faintly. "You've missed the boat, Colonel."

"Then it is impossible for us to come to an understanding?"

"There's nothing to come to an understanding about."

"Somehow I thought you'd say that." Steiner pulled on his gloves. "No hard feelings, Lomax. I respect a brave man, but I've got to do my job."

"No hard feelings," Lomax said.

The German shook hands and went out and Lomax lay back against the pillow. Nothing seemed to matter any more and he was beginning to feel sleepy as the drug started to take effect. The strange thing was that Steiner had seemed to be laughing at him and he couldn't think why. The nurse lowered the end of the table and he stared up at the light and after a while drifted into sleep.

When he awakened, he found himself lying on a stretcher in an ambulance. Two medical orderlies in field uniform were sitting beside him and he turned his head weakly and frowned. "Where am I? What's happening?"

One of them leaned across, a young, pleasant-faced boy, eyes serious under the forage cap. "There's nothing to worry about. You're going to Crete, that's all. Your leg needs a special operation."

He lay there in a daze, trying to make some sense out of it, but he found it impossible to concentrate and then the ambulance stopped and they opened the doors and took him outside.

It was early morning, grey and overcast with a light rain falling and a cold wind blew across the harbour. Thirty or forty people stood talking in little groups on the pier, mostly fishermen with one or two women hovering on the fringe.

They moved forward curiously as the two orderlies picked up the stretcher and the guards had to push a way through.

It took them a minute or two to get the stretcher down the ladder to the waiting E-boat and the orderlies laid him on the deck beside the wheelhouse and stood beside him as the sailors quickly cast off.

As the water churned at the stern and the boat pulled away from the pier, the people crowded silently forward to the edge. Lomax looked up at the line of white, meaningless faces, his vision blurring slightly, and then Katina's seemed to jump out at him.

So she was safe? There was that much to be thankful for. She was wearing a headscarf and looked exactly as he had seen her on that first night, very young, the eyes like shadows in the white face and a lump rose in his throat that threatened to choke him.

He lay there on the deck, the cold rain falling on his face and as the island faded into the mist a seagull dipped over his head and fled through the grey morning like a departing spirit.

Book Three

A Sound of Hunting

12

One Should Never Return to Anything

When he awakened, the coin was still firmly clutched in his right hand. He stared at it, a frown of bewilderment on his face, his first conscious thought that it should not be in his possession, and then he remembered.

The past and the present had become so inextricably mixed that it was difficult to make sense of either. He dropped the coin and chain on the small beside table, swung his legs to the floor and sat there trying to get his bearings.

Who am I, he thought? The Nightcomer or Hugh Lomax, residence California, scriptwriter and novelist of sorts? There was no answer or none that would suffice. He had become a stranger to himself and he got to his feet and moved across to the washstand.

There was a dull ache in his side where a foot had caught him and a bad graze on his right cheek. He pulled off his shirt and splashed lukewarm water over his face. As he started to dry himself, there was a knock at the door and Katina entered.

She was wearing the same silk headscarf and cream linen dress and she closed the door and smiled. "How do you feel?"

He grinned. "Too old for street brawls with men half my age."

She opened his suitcase, took out a clean shirt and unbuttoned it for him. "What have you been doing?"

"Going back into the past," he said. "Trying to make some sense out of things."

"A dangerous game. They say one should never return to anything."

"I'm beginning to think they're right. I'm not even sure who I am anymore."

"You are Hugh Lomax," she said, and with uncanny perception added, "The Nightcomer died a long time ago."

"I'm not so sure," he said. "He almost killed a man this afternoon."

To that she had no answer and he went on, "There's no logic to it, Katina. No answer. I've only one thing to hang on to in a world gone mad. The fact that I know that I didn't betray those who helped me."

"I know, Hugh," she said. "I believe you and so does Oliver. He wants to see you. He thinks he might be able to help. Will you come out to the villa with me?"

"What have I got to lose?" he said. "I'd like to meet him again in any case."

She crossed to the door and opened it. "I'll see you downstairs. I want a word with Anna before we leave."

He decided against a shave and finished dressing quickly. When he walked out into the hot sunlight of the square five minutes later, she was sitting behind the wheel of the jeep talking to Kytros.

As Lomax approached, the police sergeant turned and examined him critically. "You look in considerably better shape than Dimitri."

"How is he?" Lomax asked.

"When I last saw him he was having several stitches inserted into his face," Kytros said. "But don't underestimate him. It will take more than one beating to put him on his back. He's made of iron and his capacity for hate is frightening."

"Am I to take that as a warning?"

Kytros nodded gravely. "Keep off the streets at night, Mr. Lomax. There are those here who would kill you. I'd rather you didn't make it easy for them."

"My pleasure." Lomax climbed into the jeep beside Katina. "Was there anything else?"

"Perhaps the only worthwhile legacy of the German occupation is our telephone system," Kytros told him. "If you could keep me informed of your movements it would help. If I'm not at my office, the operator should be able to contact me for you."

He stepped back and Katina drove away across the square. As they turned into a side street she said, "Will you do as he asks?"

Lomax nodded. "Why not, if it keeps him happy?"

She concentrated on her driving, taking the jeep expertly through the twisting, narrow streets. There was a new bridge over the ravine outside town, its web of steel replacing the stonework of the old, but otherwise nothing seemed to have changed.

He lit a cigarette, his hands cupped against the breeze, and turned sideways so that he could look at her.

"Where's Yanni?" he said.

She smiled. "I left him in the kitchen eating his head off."

"Who with—old Maria?"

Her smile faded. "Maria died a long time ago at Fonchi. They took her when they arrested Oliver."

He groaned, remembering the old woman and her kindness, and then another thought came to him and he said slowly, "What happened to your aunt?"

"She tried to warn my uncle when they came for him. They shot her down on the stairs."

"Something else he blames me for?" Lomax asked bitterly, but she made no reply and they continued the journey in silence.

When she stopped the engine in the yard outside the stables at the rear of the villa, it was still and hot and very quiet and nothing had changed. Time stood still, the past and the present merging to touch everything with a slight edge of unreality.

As he followed her along the narrow path between the olive trees, the feeling remained, and what he found when they mounted the steps to the terrace and entered the house only strengthened the unreality.

Everything was exactly as it had been seventeen years before. The great stone fireplace, the grand piano, even the shelves filled with books, and he paused and touched them gently with one hand.

He swayed suddenly, feeling vaguely light-headed, and Katina said in alarm, "Are you all right?"

He took a deep breath and pulled himself together. "Nothing to worry about. It's just that in some strange way, time seems to have no meaning for me standing here in this room. It takes some getting used to."

She seemed about to speak, hesitated and then turned away, a slight frown on her face. She walked out into the hall and moved along the cool, whitewashed corridor that led to the north terrace.

The circular glass room was filled with a diffused light, flimsy curtains half-drawn as a filter against the strong rays of the sun. There was no sign of Van Horn, but his magnificent collection of Greek ceramics was there, the great red and black amphora still the centrepiece, aloof on its pedestal in the middle of the room.

Lomax paused to admire it then frowned and moved closer. The surface was covered by a network of fine lines. Since he had last looked upon it, it had obviously been smashed into hundreds of fragments which someone had laboriously fitted together again.

A step sounded behind him and Van Horn said, "If you're interested, it took me just over a year."

His face seemed a little thinner, the hair and moustache snow-white now, but the eyes seemed very blue in the tanned face and when Lomax took the proffered hand, the grip was surprisingly firm.

"What happened?" he said.

"To the amphora?" Van Horn shrugged. "When the

Germans came to arrest me they got a little rough. The astonishing thing was that when I returned after the war, I found the pieces in a box in the cellar. It was a good thing in a way. Piecing it together again gave me something to do during that first year. I had to take things pretty steady."

"After Fonchi?" Lomax said.

Van Horn nodded. "Let's go out on the terrace. It's rather pleasant as the evenings draw in."

Katina had withdrawn quietly and Lomax followed him outside. The view was quite breathtaking, the sun like a great orange ball dropping to meet the sea, Crete and its mountains faintly in the distance, shimmering in the heat haze.

Lomax leaned on the concrete balustrade and looked down. The cliffs dropped a good two hundred feet into a small funnel shaped inlet. From that height he was able to see quite clearly the different shades of blue and green in the water caused by the dark basalt ledges at varying depths. A thirty-foot sea-going launch floated motionless beside a stone jetty that pushed out from the bone-white sand.

Van Horn sat in a canvas chair beside a table on which stood a tray containing ice-water and several bottles and a portable typewriter.

Lomax picked up several sheets of paper, blown by the breeze, and put them back on the table. "I don't seem to have read anything new by you in quite some time."

"My dear chap, I said everything I wanted to say a long time ago." Van Horn poured gin into two glasses. "You know, we were given to understand by the Germans that you were dead. That the boat in which you were sent to Crete never reached there. What happened?"

Lomax sat down and took out a cigarette. "We ran across a Greek fishing caicque that shouldn't have been where it was and the captain decided to investigate. Unfortunately for him it turned out to be a wolf in sheep's clothing. The Special Boat Service outfit that was supposed to take us off Kyros when we'd completed our mission."

"So the E-boat was sunk? What happened to you after that?"

"The SBS commander got me to Alexandria as quickly as he could. My legs were in pretty bad shape so they flew me home to England for special treatment. I wasn't fit for active service again until the beginning of 1945. By that time things in Europe were moving pretty fast and they decided they could make better use of me in Germany."

"And why not?" Van Horn said. "After all, the Aegean was never anything more than a side show. They didn't even bother to invade Crete. When the end came the Germans simply surrendered as they did on all the islands."

"And a projected invasion of Crete was the excuse for the whole Kyros operation," Lomax said. "Presumably you think the whole thing was a waste of time?"

Van Horn looked mildly surprised. "Did I ever pretend anything else? Things were all very romantic here in the Aegean with your landings by night and your legalised brigandry, but don't let's pretend it had the slightest effect on the course of the war."

Blind, unreasoning anger sparked inside Lomax. "It's a pity Joe Boyd and one or two more I could mention aren't around to hear you say that."

"I could give you a few names myself," Van Horn said calmly. "Old Maria, Alexias's wife and several more. Innocent bystanders who hardly knew what it was all about. Fonchi was bad enough, but what about the women and young girls like Katina who were sent to the troop brothels in Greece? They were the real victims."

His voice moved on, but Lomax didn't hear it. He closed his eyes and was sucked into a dark vacuum of quiet. The agony was almost physical, a hard ball that rose into his throat, threatening to choke him, and he lurched to the balustrade and was violently sick.

He stayed there for a little while, staring down into the void, and slowly, sounds came back to him and he was aware of Van Horn at his elbow holding out a glass.

As the contents burned their way down into his stomach, Van Horn said quietly, "I'm sorry, I thought you knew."

"The one thing she omitted to tell me," Lomax whispered.

Van Horn put a hand gently on his shoulder and then returned to his chair and Lomax lit a cigarette and stayed there staring blindly into space.

After a while he turned and said quietly, "Katina tells me you're the only other person she knows who believes I didn't betray you all to Steiner."

Van Horn poured himself another drink. "That's right."

"May I ask why?"

Van Horn shrugged. "Let's just say it didn't seem in character."

"And you think that a sufficient reason?"

"I'm a professional writer, remember. People are my business."

Lomax sat down again at a table. "Tell me what happened when they arrrested you."

"A rather officious young officer arrived with a squad of men and searched the house without giving me any explanation. That's when the amphora got smashed. Afterwards, they took me to headquarters to see Steiner. He simply said that he had information to the effect that I'd harboured you and Boyd. Naturally, I told him I didn't know what he was talking about."

"And when was it first suggested that I'd given him the information?"

"I first heard it about a month later from one of the guards at the town gaol."

"They didn't send you to Fonchi straight away then?"

"I was in prison here for three months before they transferred me. Most of the others were already there when I arrived."

"Including Alexias?"

"He was never at Fonchi. They sent him direct to the Gestapo prison in Athens. I suppose they thought they could squeeze him dry in time. They knew he'd been working with the EOK in Crete."

"But why did they keep you here in the town gaol after the others had left?"

"That was Steiner's doing. He knew my health wasn't good and the garrison doctor told him I wouldn't last three months at Fonchi. I think he was trying to do the best he could for me."

"Why should he?" Lomax demanded bluntly.

"He liked me, it was as simple as that." Van Horn shrugged. "We played chess every week, remember. When I needed them, he obtained scarce medical supplies that saved many lives. He was ruthless, even cold-blooded, but he was not a bad man."

"Then why the change of heart after three months?"

"There was none. He left the island on an E-boat one morning bound for a military conference on Crete. Like you, he was never heard of again. His successor had me transferred to Fonchi as soon as he took over. I was there until the German surrender in Greece the following year."

"That garrison doctor was pretty wide of the mark when he said you wouldn't last three months," Lomax said.

His challenge was unmistakable and the fact of it lay between them like a sword. Out of the silence Van Horn said calmly, "There would appear to be some doubt in your mind as to the truth of my story. Perhaps I can convince you with something a little more concrete than words."

He stood up, unbuttoned his cream linen beach shirt and turned. From his shoulders to the base of the spine, his back was a mass of scar tissue, great raised weals crossing each other to form an ugly web that could have had only one possible cause.

He pulled on his shirt again. "Not very pleasant, eh? Fifty lashes for striking a guard and that was mild compared to what they did to some people."

"And you survived that?" Lomax said slowly.

Van Horn started to button his shirt. "I reached rock-bottom, Lomax. The ultimate in degradation. It's a funny thing, but when you're that low, you become so full of hate for the people who've put you there that it gives you new life. I swore I'd live to walk out through the gates of that place. As a matter of fact they had to carry me, but at least I was alive."

Lomax got to his feet and went to the balustrade and stood there, seeing again in his mind's eye the scars criss-crossing Van Horn's back, thinking of those who had died and of Katina and her own private agony.

After a moment, Van Horn moved beside him and said softly, "I'm afraid you'll have to look elsewhere for your traitor."

"Any suggestions?" Lomax said.

Van Horn shook his head and sighed. "Even if I knew, I'm not sure that I'd tell you."

For a long moment Lomax looked down into the fine face and the blue eyes so full of compassion and then he turned quickly and went back into the house.

13

To the Other End of Time

He went down the steps from the terrace and moved through the garden, conscious of its freshness after the heat of the day. The sky was an angry red towards the horizon, the cypress trees by the wall etched against it like black lace, but just above them, the crimson faded into a dark blue vault in which a single evening star was already shining.

He could hear the splash of water from a fountain hidden somewhere among the bushes and moving on through a narrow gate, found himself standing at the top of the cliffs.

At that moment Yanni came over the edge and cannoned into him. He glanced up in surprise and then grinned impudently. "Oh, it's you, Mr. Lomax."

"And where are you off to in such a hurry?" Lomax demanded.

"To the kitchen." The boy's grin widened. "Katina's asked me to tell the cook she can start to get supper ready."

"Is she on the beach?" Lomax said.

Yanni nodded. "I've been helping her to get the boat ready. She and Mr. Van Horn are sailing to Crete on Saturday. Katina says I can crew for them if I behave myself."

"See that you do." Lomax ruffled the boy's hair and Yanni grinned and darted through the archway towards the house.

The beach was reached by a series of stone steps that

zig-zagged in a haphazard way across the face of the cliff. Lomax was sweating slightly when he reached the bottom. He started along the jetty and saw her at the water's edge half-way round the curve of the bay.

She was standing knee-deep in the sea and held the skirt of her frock bunched in front of her with one hand, her face turned towards the sunset.

There was something indomitable about her, something eternal with its roots deep in this ancient land as she stood there, the proud curves of her body dark against the sky, the sea spilling orange fire around her bare thighs.

She turned her head and saw him and his throat went dry. It was with almost a sense of revelation, of wonder, that he realised she was beautiful.

She smiled. "You and Oliver didn't talk long."

"Why didn't you tell me, Katina?" he said simply.

For a long moment they gazed at each other and then she waded out of the water and crossed the beach to a hollow in the sand surrounded by a horseshoe of boulders. Her shoes and a towel lay on an old travelling rug and she sat down and started to dry her legs.

Lomax crouched beside her and lit a cigarette. After a moment she held out her hand. "Do you mind?"

He gave her the cigarette without speaking and there was silence between them while she smoked it.

After a while she sighed and tossed it away. "What do you want me to say? That my life was ruined? That each day was a torment?"

"Wasn't it?"

"It was all so long ago that it might have happened to someone else," she said. "In any case, I was lucky. I became pregnant after a couple of months and they turned me out to fend for myself."

"And the child?"

"I had a miscarriage." She shrugged. "It wouldn't have lived anyway. In those days half Greece was starving."

"I'm sorry, Katina," he said. "You'll never know how sorry."

"But there's nothing to be sorry about."

"Isn't there? Remember what Father John said that day at The Little Ship? How men like me always left other people to pay for our glory?"

She shook her head and said firmly. "Only the war was to blame. I told you once that it was a dark dream in which nothing that happened made any sense."

"And from which some people never manage to awaken."

"You mean my uncle?" She sighed. "Yes, I'm afraid he's never been able to forget. He lives on his own too much and broods."

"On his own?"

"At the farm. He's leased it from me ever since the war. He's come to spend an increasing amount of time there over the years. It isn't good for him."

"Surely he must employ a housekeeper and labourers to work in the vineyard."

"Only during the day. At night he prefers to be alone."

"What about The Little Ship?"

"He took Nikoli into partnership years ago. He and Dimitri Paros run it between them."

Lomax frowned. "Why Dimitri?"

She shrugged. "My uncle has always felt a responsibility towards him. His father was one of those who died at Fonchi."

"And they all hate me," he said. "All except you. Why, Katina? Why should you be different?"

She pushed herself up and said lightly, "But you have given me no reason to hate you."

She stood looking out to sea as the sun finally dipped beneath the horizon and Lomax got to his feet and moved to her shoulder.

"Why did you never marry?" he said softly. "A girl like you must have had offers."

She turned very slowly and in the weird orange light reflected from the sea she might have been Helen gazing on Troy burning and never more beautiful.

Her eyes were dark pools a man could never fathom. When she whispered his name and took a step forward they came together naturally and easily. Her hands pulled his head down as her mouth sought his and then he lifted her in his arms and laid her down on the rug.

She was crying, her face wet with tears, he was aware of that and then a great wind seemed to gather them up and carry them off to the other end of time.

As they went through the garden to the house they walked hand-in-hand like children. Katina's linen dress was badly crumpled and stained with salt water and Lomax chuckled and kissed her gently on one cheek. "You'd better change before supper. We don't want to shock Oliver in his old age."

They moved through the sitting room into the hall and paused at the bottom of the stairs. "I think I'll take a shower as well," she said. "I'll see you in half an hour."

He nodded. "I'll be on the terrace with Van Horn."

She kissed him briefly and turned away and he stayed there, aware that her fragrance still lingered in the air around him, feeling curiously sad.

For a little while he had managed to escape from the world of hate and violence into which he had been plunged. But what he had just experienced on the beach had been a brief foretaste of a happiness he could only have if he solved a seventeen-year-old mystery. He was beginning to doubt whether that was possible.

Van Horn was sitting on the terrace in the same canvas chair smoking a cigarette and looking out to sea with a pair of night glasses.

"Ah, there you are," he said. "Enjoy your walk?"

"I went down to the beach," Lomax told him. "Quite a boat you've got there."

Van Horn nodded. "Comes in very handy. It means I can get across to Crete when the mood hits me. The mail boat only calls here once a week."

"I'm only too well aware of that fact," Lomax said.

He leaned against the balustrade and looked out over the darkening sea and after a while, Van Horn said softly, "Why did you come back, Lomax? Why now after all these years?"

Lomax shrugged. "I felt like a change, it was that simple."

"But nothing ever is," Van Horn said.

Knowing at once that he was right, Lomax frowned, trying to get it straight in his own mind. After a moment he said, "I seemed to have taken a wrong turning somewhere."

"You wanted to be a writer, didn't you?"

Lomax nodded. "Oh, I became one all right. Not the great novelist I'd imagined or anything like that, but I've done all right in the film game."

"Learning to compromise is one of the hardest things in life."

Lomax laughed harshly. "In my case it seemed at times as if life had done the compromising. I reached a state in which my mornings carried a permanent taste of dead yesterdays. I thought that if I came back to the Aegean, took some time off to think, that I might find where I'd gone wrong, begin again."

Van Horn sighed. "Isn't that what we all want to do and never can? We wouldn't make the same mistakes twice—we'd simply make fresh ones." He smiled softly. "There's an old Greek saying: 'For every joy the Gods give two sorrows.' We must accept life as it is, Lomax, and work from there."

Lomax shook his head. "Too fatalistic for my taste. A

man must be willing to fight back when the going gets rough."

"Presumably you intend to do just that?"

Lomax nodded. "I'm fully aware that I have some sort of moral responsibility for starting what happened here, but I didn't pull the trigger on these people. I don't see why I should carry the cross for the person who did."

"But you've nothing to go on. You don't even know what you're looking for."

"It's quite simple really," Lomax said. "I'm looking for the member of the original group who doesn't fit into the general pattern. The person who obviously benefited by his treachery."

"Or his weakness or fear, have you considered that?" Van Horn shook his head. "It won't work, Lomax. Every member of the group suffered in one way or another. Some died, the rest saw the war out in Fonchi, and we all squatted in that Hell together. No one received special treatment, I can assure you."

"Except Alexias," Lomax said.

"As I think I mentioned earlier, they sent him to Gestapo Headquarters in Athens for special treatment of another sort."

"But why should they?" Lomax demanded. "They knew he'd worked with me and with the EOK on Crete, but it's highly unlikely he could have told them anything about the general set-up there that they didn't already know. Under the rules of the Geneva Convention they were quite entitled to shoot him as a spy and yet they didn't."

"On the other hand, they usually executed Special Air Service officers when they caught them and failed to do so in your own case."

Lomax nodded slowly. "That's the one thing I've never understood. Why Steiner didn't have me shot. They couldn't have been saving me for Crete because the policy was to hold a public execution in front of the local populace where they caught you."

"I might add that if you're looking for someone who doesn't fit into the general pattern there's always Katina," Van Horn said calmly.

Lomax looked at him in astonishment. "For God's sake be sensible. We know exactly what happened there."

"We only have her word for it. If you suspect her uncle then you must logically suspect her also." Lomax frowned and sat down in the opposite chair and Van Horn continued. "Another thing. Even if Alexias did betray us, that still doesn't explain how the Germans got on to him in the first place."

And there was the one great flaw. Lomax sighed heavily. "You're right of course."

"I'm sorry," Van Horn said gently. "But it had to be said. "What will you do now?"

Lomax got to his feet. "I still think it's time I had a word with Alexias. After all, in a manner of speaking, he's at the heart of things."

"Do you think he'll see you?"

"I don't see why not. Katina tells me he lives out at the farm on his own. If I simply turn up there, he won't have much choice, will he?"

"You're aware, of course, that he may be praying for you to put in an appearance? That you could be running your head into a noose?"

"That *had* occurred to me," Lomax said calmly.

Van Horn got to his feet and moved to the balustrade. For a moment he stood there looking out to sea and then he turned. "I can't say I approve of all this, Lomax. Frankly, I don't think it really matters any more, but if I can help in any way, I will. You're welcome to borrow the jeep for a start."

Lomax shook his head. "Thanks all the same, but I could do with some time to work things out. I think I'll walk over the mountain."

"Can't I persuade you to stay for supper?"

"I don't think so. For one thing, I don't want Katina

to get involved too much in this business. If she knows I intend seeing her uncle, she might try to prevent me."

"What shall I tell her?"

Lomax shrugged. "Anything you like. Say that I'll be in touch. That I want to think things over on my own."

Van Horn looked as if he intended to argue, but Lomax turned quickly, went through the house and out into the garden. As he moved towards the main gates, someone called his name and Yanni emerged from the yard.

"Aren't you staying for supper?"

Lomax shook his head. "I've got pressing business, son. Something that can't wait. Tell Katina how sorry I am."

Yanni's young face was solemn. "You looking for trouble again, Mr. Lomax?"

Lomax grinned. "It's usually the other way round. You go back in the house now. I'll see you tomorrow."

He moved across the road and started up the hillside. It was that quiet period half-way between evening and night and strangely still. He could hear a dog barking in the distance and the scent of woodsmoke drifted on a small wind from some shepherd's hut.

When he stopped to rest, he leaned against a boulder and lit a cigarette. He had been aware for some time that he was being followed and he moved back into the shadows and waited. A moment later there was a rattle of stones and Yanni came cautiously forward.

He paused, obviously undecided, and Lomax moved from behind the boulder and tapped him on the shoulder. "And where might you be going?"

Yanni smiled sheepishly. "I didn't mean no harm, Mr. Lomax. I thought you might get into trouble again like this afternoon."

"Well you thought wrong," Lomax said. "Does Katina know you're here?"

"If I'd told her, she'd have wanted to come too."

Lomax turned him round firmly and gave him a push.

"Now you get back down to the villa before she starts worrying about you."

The boy moved away. He paused once and looked round, but Lomax hardened his heart and waved him on and he disappeared reluctantly into the dark shadow of the ravine. For a moment Lomax stood there, a smile touching his mouth, and then he turned and started to climb again.

When he moved over the rim of the plateau near the top of the mountain and looked again upon the Tomb of Achilles, night was at hand.

He stood in the desolate light of gloaming and the mountain was tipped with orange fire. Below him the sea was black with depth, purple and grey near the shore, and the lights of the villa seemed very far away.

The beauty of it was too much for a man and he felt strangely sad and drained of all emotion and then the fire on the mountain died and night enveloped him. A small wind whispered between the pillars of the temple and there was only the silence.

He turned cold and a thrill of elemental fear moved inside him. Here on top of this mountain, standing amid the ruins of an ancient race, he was faced with the silence of eternity and the realisation of his own insignificance in the general scheme of things. Whatever a man did came to nothing in the final analysis.

That being so, he could only do what had to be done and hope for the best. He crossed the plateau and started down towards the other side of the island.

14

A Fine Night for Dying

The moon was rising as he went down the hill through the olive trees and he could taste the salt on the wind. The farm was shrouded in the darkness of the hollow, still and quiet with no light showing anywhere, and he ducked under a fence and moved cautiously across the yard.

An old and battered pick-up truck, relic of the war years, was parked by the porch. The radiator was still warm when he touched it and he stood for a moment, a slight frown on his face, and then mounted the steps to the porch and opened the door.

There was a slight eerie creaking from the hinges, but no other sound. He moved into the kitchen, eyes probing the darkness, and paused suddenly, aware with complete certainty that he was not alone.

A foot scraped on a flagstone and Dimitri Paros said from the shadows, "Come right in, Mr. Lomax. We hoped you'd call."

Lomax took a quick step backwards and something exploded in the pit of his stomach, doubling him over. He sank to his knees and keeled slowly over on to one side.

A lamp was turned on, flooding the room with light, and he lay with his knees drawn up, fighting for breath while his wrists were tied behind his back.

He was aware of voices speaking together in Greek and the sound of laughter and then someone grabbed him by the lapels and hauled him to his feet.

There were two others besides Dimitri and stamped in the same mould, young fishermen in shabby reefer jackets and patched jeans. One of them was shaking with excitement and the other kept wiping sweat from his forehead with the back of his hand.

Dimitri's head was heavily bandaged, his face drawn with pain. "You're going to die, Englishman," he said, and his eyes were like stone. "For making a fool of me in front of my friends with your dirty tricks and for sending my father to his death in Fonchi camp."

Lomax was managing to draw air into his tortured lungs once more, but his mouth was so parched that he found difficulty in speaking. He moistened dry lips and croaked, "I didn't send your father to his death, or anyone else. He was a brave man for whom I had only respect."

Dimitri struck him back-handed across the face. "You are not fit to speak of him." He turned to the other two. "Get him into the truck."

They ran Lomax out through the door, bundled him into the cab of the old truck and pushed him down on the floor. One of them climbed behind the wheel and Dimitri and the other walked round to the far side.

Lomax twisted on to his front and as the headlights were switched on, found himself looking straight at Dimitri. The *bouzouki* player produced a Beretta automatic of the type issued to Italian officers during the war and handed it to the other man.

"If he gives you any trouble between here and town, shoot him."

"What do we do when we've got rid of him?" his companion said.

"Come straight back to the farm. I'll be waiting to hear the good news." Dimitri turned to Lomax. "Sorry I can't be in at the kill, but I've got other business to attend to. Riki here and Nikita will look after you just fine.

They've got almost as good a reason for hating you as I have."

"You'll never get away with this," Lomax said.

Dimitri spat full in his face. "That's for luck, Englishman. You're going to need it."

He stepped back as Riki clambered up into the passenger seat and the truck moved away over the uneven surface of the yard. As they turned on to the track, Nikita moved into top gear and the roar of the engine filled the small cab.

Lomax twisted to one side and looked up. In the light from the instrument panel Nikita seemed almost subhuman, the bones of his face standing out in sharp relief as sweat dripped from his pointed chin.

Riki, who had been smoking a cigarette, tossed it out of the window and started to sing, and the roaring of the engine drowned his voice so that as his mouth opened and closed no sound seemed to come out.

There was an impossible, nightmarish quality to the whole thing and for the first time Lomax began to feel afraid. "Listen to me!" he shouted desperately.

If either of them heard him above the noise of the engine, they made no sign. The truck bounced over a ridge in the road, rolling him over on his face again, and as panic moved inside him he turned on his back and cried at the top of his voice, "For God's sake listen to me!"

The effect was almost miraculous. The truck skidded to a halt and Nikita cut the engine in the same moment. They sat looking down at him, neither of them saying anything, waiting for him to speak, and Lomax said, "This is madness. Killing me will earn you nothing but grief."

"You have a better idea" Riki asked calmly.

"I'm a rich man," Lomax said. "My life is worth a great deal to me."

The very oppressiveness of the silence which followed

told him that he had said the wrong thing. With a sudden curse, Riki raised a foot and pushed hard down on the unprotected neck. Lomax started to choke and a few seconds later the pressure was released.

"You ever hear of a man called George Samos?" Riki demanded.

Lomax nodded, feeling suddenly cold, realising what was to come. "I knew a shepherd by that name. He helped me when I was here during the war."

"He was our uncle," Riki said. "Our father's brother. The Germans hunted him down up there on the mountain and shot him like a dog."

"You think money could pay for that, Englishman?" Nikita demanded.

There was nothing Lomax could say, nothing they would have been prepared to listen to. He lay there helplessly while Riki produced a large red bandanna and quickly gagged him with it, and Nikita started the engine again and drove away.

He was aware that they had entered the town because the truck had to slow to negotiate the narrow streets, and by turning his head slightly he could look up through the windscreen at the roofs of the houses.

When the truck finally rolled to a halt and Nikita cut the engine, Riki jumped to the ground first. He pulled Lomax out after him and held the Beretta under his nose.

"Do exactly as you're told," he said. "Don't make me use this thing."

They were parked at the end of the breakwater which was farthest away from the pier. It was dark and lonely, the only sound the lapping of the water against the pilings of the old wooden jetty below. When a café door was opened somewhere in the distance the music and laughter might have been coming from another planet, and Lomax shivered as they went down a flight of stone steps to the jetty.

The old forty-foot diesel launch moored at the far end was festooned with nets still damp from the day's labour, and stank of fish, the deck slippery with their scales. They made him lie face down on the nets while they tied his ankles, and then Nikita went aft and returned with a pile of heavy chains which he dropped on the deck with a clatter.

Riki turned Lomax over and squatted beside him. "For you, Englishman. There's a place we know a couple of miles out. Dark and quiet and very deep. You'll have it all to yourself."

He patted Lomax on the cheek, stood up and turned to his brother. "I'll take her out. You see to the moorings."

He went into the wheelhouse and Nikita cast off aft and moved into the prow. For a moment he was out of sight and Lomax swung on to his side, straining desperately at the ropes which bound him, but he was wasting his time.

The jetty lay quiet and deserted in the diffused, yellow light of a solitary lamp. There was no one to help him now, and then, somewhere in the shadows, a can was knocked on to its side and rolled across the deck with a clatter.

As Lomax twisted to look behind him, Nikita hurried aft, a frown of alarm on his face. "What the hell's going on?" he demanded, and then a large, black-and-white cat moved out of the shadows and rubbed itself against his leg.

He picked it up and shook it affectionately. "Old devil, you had my heart in my mouth."

As he put the cat down again and turned away, the engine burst into life, shattering the calm of the night, and the boat moved away from the jetty. A few moments later they passed the light at the end of the pier and turned out to sea.

Fog lifted from the water, giving it a peculiar luminosity and the sky was a jewel-studded delight. As Riki increased speed, his brother moved to the rail and stood there, allowing the spray to fall across his face.

He stayed there for quite a while and then turned and lit a cigarette, the match flaring in his cupped hands, momentarily illuminating the strong-boned face.

He flicked it into the sea and looked down at Lomax. "A night to thank God for, Englishman. A fine night for dying."

His teeth gleamed in the darkness and he walked away, humming to himself, and disappeared into the wheelhouse. In spite of the gag Lomax heaved a sigh of relief. For quite some time he had been aware that the cat had not been responsible for knocking over the can as they left the jetty and that someone crouched in the darkness behind the pile of nets.

He started to push himself backwards, and as hands started to untie the knots of the bandanna, Yanni Melos whispered into his ear, "Take it easy, Mr. Lomax. Let's get this off first."

Lomax spat out the gag and gulped in a mouthful of fresh salt air. He didn't waste time on pointless questions. "If you've got a knife, you'd better move fast, son. He'll be back any minute."

There was a sharp click as the boy pressed the button of a spring knife, and a second later Lomax was rubbing his wrists, wincing with pain as the blood started to move again.

As Yanni sliced through the rope which bound his ankles, the engine was cut and the boat started to slow down. The boy moved back into the shadows and Lomax said quietly, "Stay out of this. I don't want you to get hurt."

There was a burst of laughter and Nikita emerged from the wheelhouse and came towards them. He squatted beside Lomax and grinned. "Not long now, Englishman."

He stiffened suddenly, the smile leaving his face, and

as he leaned forward Lomax slashed him across the wind-pipe with the edge of his hand.

Nikita gave a terrible, choking cry and went over backwards to writhe on the deck, hands tearing at his throat. Riki emerged from the wheelhouse at the same moment, the Beretta ready in his hand. He loosed off a quick shot and Lomax did the only possible thing and went over the rail in a shallow dive.

As the water closed above him he was already turning to swim down and under the boat, the keel scraping his back painfully. He surfaced on the other side beside a short ladder of the type used by sponge divers and hung there for a moment to catch his breath.

The water was surprisingly cold and he was shivering as he went up the ladder. Riki stood with his back turned peering down into the sea, and as Lomax started to climb over the rail, Yanni moved from behind the pile of nets.

His arm rose, the blade gleaming like silver in the moonlight, and Riki chose that precise moment to turn. He swayed out of harm's way then twisted the knife from the boy's hand and threw it into the sea. As Yanni backed away, he went after him, face contorted with rage, the Beretta extended threateningly.

A six-foot gaff used for hauling in the big fish hung from a hook beside the wheelhouse. It was the only possible weapon and Lomax grabbed it and moved forward quickly.

"Here I am, Riki!" he called.

The Greek glanced sideways, jaw going slack in astonishment, and then he started to turn, bringing the gun to bear. Lomax lunged awkwardly with the gaff and the blade sliced through the heavy reefer jacket into the right armpit.

Riki screamed, dropping the gun at once, and staggered backwards, jerking the gaff from Lomax's grasp. He pulled it from his armpit and sank down on the pile of nets, moaning in pain.

Yanni stumbled across to the rail and leaned over the side, his small body heaving, and Lomax picked up the Beretta and moved after him. The boy turned, wiping his mouth with the back of one hand, trying hard to hold back his tears and failing.

"I thought you were dead," he said. "I thought you'd gone down for good."

Lomax pushed him gently towards the wheelhouse. "Go inside and wait for me. I won't be long."

He pushed the Beretta into the waistband of his pants and went into the galley. It was dark and airless, but he managed to find a towel and went back on deck.

Riki crouched beside his brother who lay very still, head turned to one side, the whites of his eyes gleaming in the diffused yellow light from the wheelhouse.

Lomax dropped to one knee, folded the towel into a thick pad and held it out. "If you hold this under your arm as tightly as you can you might live long enough to see a doctor."

Riki's face was sickly yellow in the lamplight, the eyes fixed and staring. "He's dead," he said stupidly. "My brother is dead."

Lomax lifted the man's arm away from his body and pushed the padded towel into position. Riki made no attempt to stop him. He sat there beside the body of his brother holding his damaged arm against his side and Lomax turned wearily away and went into the wheelhouse.

He leaned against the door and closed his eyes and it was as if he was alone and the darkness moved in on him, pushing against his body with a terrible weightless pressure. He was lost, alone in that darkness groping for a light and then a hand tugged at his damp sleeve and he opened his eyes and looked down at Yanni.

The boy's face was white and anxious and Lomax patted him reassuringly. "It's all right, Yanni. I'm not as young as I used to be, that's all."

But there was more to it than that—much more. He glanced down through the window at Riki crouched beside the body of his brother and turned away hurriedly, sick to his stomach.

His hands were shaking when he pressed the starter. The engine coughed once asthmatically and then roared into life, and he took the boat round in a long sweeping curve and said, "Now you can tell me how you managed to turn up when you did."

"I followed you over the mountain to the farm instead of going back to the villa when you told me," Yanni explained. "When they brought you outside and put you in the truck, I climbed on to the spare wheel at the rear."

"You must have had a pretty rough ride," Lomax said.

"It could have been worse." The boy shrugged. "I wanted to go for Kytros, but I didn't like to leave you. I couldn't walk along the jetty because of the lamp, so I swam out from the beach and climbed over the stern. That's when I knocked the can over." He hesitated and said diffidently. "Did I do right, Mr. Lomax?"

Lomax grinned down at him. "I'm beginning to wonder how I ever managed without you."

The fog that curled up from the surface of the water had thickened a little, but within a few minutes he saw the harbour lights on the port side and altered course.

As they passed the end of the pier, Yanni moved out on deck and stood ready with one of the mooring lines. Lomax reduced speed and cut the engine when they were a few yards from the jetty. He had miscalculated slightly and the boat drifted broadside on against the pilings with a splintering of wood, the shock sending him staggering across the wheelhouse.

When he moved out on deck, Yanni was already on the jetty expertly hooking the line over an iron bollard.

He grinned. "How long since you brought a boat into harbour, Mr. Lomax?"

"I got us here," Lomax said. "That's all that counts.

How far is it to the police station?"

"Just around the corner," Yanni said. "A couple of minutes, that's all. Shall I get Sergeant Kytros?"

Lomax nodded. "I'll wait here."

A hollow booming echoed across the water as the boy ran along the wooden planking of the jetty to the wharf and disappeared into the darkness.

When Lomax turned, he saw that Riki was on his feet. He stood looking down at the body of his brother, legs braced apart, damaged arm held firmly against his side.

"Who sicked you and your brother and Dimitri on to me?" Lomax said. "Was it Alexias Pavlo?"

Riki looked up slowly. In the yellow light of the lamp his eyes were black holes, the face glistening with sweat, a mask of pain.

He said nothing and yet his hatred lay between them like a living thing and Lomax shivered as if somewhere, someone had walked over his grave. A small wind lifted from the water, slicing through his damp clothing and he turned, stepped over the rail and walked along the jetty.

When he reached the wharf he hesitated, knowing that the sensible thing to do was to wait for Kytros, to let him handle things. And then he thought of Dimitri waiting out there at the farm for news that he was dead and anger moved inside him. He climbed into the truck and a moment later drove rapidly away.

A solitary light greeted him from the darkness of the hollow when he took the truck down towards the farmhouse. He braked to a halt, cut the engine and sat there looking towards the porch. After a moment, he jumped down to the ground and moved up the steps.

He took the Beretta from his waistband, held it against his right thigh with the safety catch off and went in. The kitchen was in darkness, but a thin strip of light showed at the bottom of the door leading to the living room.

He stood there, conscious of the uncanny stillness, the

absolute quiet, and somewhere in the distance thunder rumbled menacingly. He opened the door and stepped into the living room in one smooth movement.

A fire crackled on the hearth and a lamp stood on the table in the centre of the room, its yellow glow beating the shadows back into their corners.

And then he noticed the bottle lying on the sheepskin rug where it had fallen. Red wine spilling across the floor like blood, reached out towards the legs that protruded from the shadows behind one of the great wing-backed chairs beside the fire.

Dimitri Paros stared up at the ceiling, eyes fixed for eternity, a half-smile frozen into place. The horn-handle of a gutting knife jutted from beneath his chin, the long blade passing through the roof of the mouth into the brain.

In one hand he still clutched a wine-glass, its contents spilled on the floor beside him, and Lomax pushed the Beretta into his waistband and dropped to one knee.

When he touched the white face with the back of one hand, he found it still warm. He was only just dead, that much was obvious, and Lomax sighed and started to get to his feet.

A slight breeze touched the back of his neck and the door creaked. A familiar voice said, "Please to stand very still."

Alexias Pavlo moved into the room leaning heavily on his cane, a Mauser clutched firmly in his other hand. He removed the Beretta, slipping it into his pocket, and glanced down at Dimitri.

When he looked again at Lomax, his face was dark with vengeance and as implacable, hewn out of stone.

"Now I will see you hang, Captain Lomax," he said.

15

A Prospect of Gallows

The cell was small and bare with whitewashed walls and illuminated by a single bulb. There was a small, barred window, a washbasin and the bunk on which he was lying.

The door was reinforced with bands of iron and a tiny grille gave a limited view of the corridor. From the direction of the office he could hear the low murmur of voices.

He wrapped a blanket around his body against the bitter cold that seeped through his damp clothing and smoked one of the cigarettes Kytros had given him.

Through the bars of the window he could see the blue-black night sky and a scattering of stars and in the distance thunder rumbled again. He got to his feet and moved to the window and far out to sea lightning flickered below the horizon.

A step sounded in the corridor. As he turned, Stavrou the gaoler, a tall, thick-set man in crumpled khaki uniform, unlocked the door.

Lomax dropped the blanket on the bed and moved into the corridor. "Now what?"

"The sergeant's been having a word with Father John," Stavrou said. "The old man wants to have a word with you before he goes."

The office was a place of shadows, its only illumination the green shaded lamp on the desk. Father John sat beside it, a hand to his brow, as Kytros stood at the window. As Lomax paused in the doorway, the old man turned his head sharply.

For a long moment there was silence between them and then he pushed himself to his feet. "Is there anything I can do for you?"

"I shouldn't imagine so," Lomax said.

"Sergeant Kytros tells me you have accused Alexias Pavlo in this matter," the priest said calmly.

"And you don't think him capable, I suppose?" Lomax said.

"Of killing?" Father John shrugged. "The Devil is in each one of us. However, this evening, Alexias Pavlo was where he has been every Thursday night for years. Playing chess at my home until nine-thirty."

"That still gave him enough time," Lomax said stubbornly.

The old man shook his head. "I hardly think so."

At that moment a stone rattled against the shutters that covered the window. "They're beginning to get nasty," Kytros said.

Father John and Lomax moved to join him. Through the narrow slats of the shutters Lomax saw twenty or thirty people standing in small groups, some talking, others just looking towards the police station.

"What do they want?" he said.

"You, I should imagine," Kytros replied calmly.

"It will be a long time before the island sees the end of this night's work," Father John said, pulling his cloak over his shoulders.

"And naturally, I'm to blame?" Lomax said.

"To say with certainty where responsibility lies for anything in this life is difficult," the old man said. "I am only sure of this: Two men are dead. You should have left on the boat, Mr. Lomax. I see now that we should have compelled you to go."

Lomax sat down and helped himself to a cigarette from a packet on the desk. "It would have been so damned convenient for you all, Father. You could have gone on pretending that I was to blame. That the man responsible for so much evil wasn't one of your own people."

The old man looked at him, a slight puzzled frown on his face. For a moment he seemed about to speak and then appeared to think better of it.

He turned to Kytros. "I must go now. I've still to visit the parents of Nikita Samos."

"Thank you for coming, Father," Kytros said.

"I'll order the people outside to go to their homes," the old man went on. "If you need me later, don't hesitate to call."

He turned again to Lomax, hesitated and then went to the door. As it closed behind him, Kytros moved to the window. After a while, he gave a grunt of satisfaction.

"Are they going?" Lomax asked.

"For the moment, but they'll be back."

Stavrou busied himself at a table in the shadows where a pot bubbled on a small spirit stove. He filled two cups and brought them to the desk and Lomax inhaled the fragrance of good coffee. It was hot and scalding, filling him with new life, and he sighed with pleasure and lit another cigarette.

Kytros sat on the other side of the desk. He inserted a Turkish cigarette into a plain silver holder and lit it. He leaned back so that he was on the edge of the circle of light, his face in shadow.

"One thing puzzles me," he said. "Dimitri Paros liked to be in at the kill where most things were concerned, yet he chose to forgo the pleasure of personally eliminating a man he hated. I wonder why?"

"He said he had business to take care of."

"It must have been important."

He opened his drawer and took out the Beretta and the gutting knife which had killed Dimitri. It was of common pattern, the handle of black horn bound with brass and slightly curved. When he pressed the button with his thumb, a nine-inch blade appeared as if by magic.

He pushed it back into place and frowned. "Rather an unusual way to stab a man to death, wouldn't you say?"

"An old commando trick," Lomax said. "Here, I'll show you."

He took the knife and stood, holding it concealed in the palm of his right hand against his thigh. His arm swung upwards suddenly, the blade jumping out of his hand like a snake's tongue. He dropped it point first into the desk and sat down again.

"It's a convenient way of killing a man at close quarters from the front. Death is instantaneous because the blade penetrates the brain."

"And this was the method used to kill Dimitri Paros?"

"I'm sure of it. There was still a smile on his face. You must have noticed that yourself. He was killed by someone he knew well and I'd like to point out that he'd hardly have been smiling at me."

"A good point," Kytros admitted, "though I wouldn't have described it as a pleasant smile."

"There was nothing pleasant about the bastard," Lomax said. "Another thing, if I'd wanted to kill him, why use the knife when I had the Beretta?"

Kytros sighed. "A confusing business, Mr. Lomax. If only you'd waited for me at the wharf. Things could have been so different."

"The story of my life. What happens now?"

"There are various loose ends. The autopsy for instance. Doctor Spanos is doing it now. Afterwards . . ."

Stavrou moved forward swinging his keys and Lomax said bitterly, "In other words I'm still number one on the list."

"I'm afraid so," Kytros said.

"Have it your way. Just remember I'm a British citizen."

Kytros nodded. "I'll radio Crete. They'll notify your embassy in Athens at once. Is there anything else?"

"I could do with a change of clothing. I'm still rather

damp and it's pretty cold in that cell."

"I'll see what I can do," Kytros said. "Now, you must excuse me. I have many things to attend to."

Stavrou took Lomax back to the cell and locked him in. When he had gone, Lomax hitched the blanket about his shoulders and sat on the bed, his back against the wall.

If only he'd waited for Kytros on the wharf. But it was too late for that kind of talk now. He was trapped in a web of circumstantial evidence, already judged and condemned.

Steps sounded in the corridor. As he turned to the door Stavrou's face appeared at the grille. He opened the door and tossed a woollen sweater on the bed. "Something to be going on with."

Lomax peeled off his jacket and reached for the sweater. As he pulled it over his head, there was a movement in the shadows and Katina moved forward.

Her face was very white, the eyes dark pools. They stood there in a private world of their own saying nothing and Stavrou cleared his throat. "Five minutes, that's all."

The door closed, the key turned in the lock and they were alone. She raised a hand and gently touched his face. "Are you all right? They haven't hurt you?"

"A few bruises. Nothing to speak of."

And then he noticed that she had been weeping and drew her down on to the bed. "What is it, Katina?"

"I went to The Little Ship to ask my uncle to help, but he refused to see me," she said. "Nikoli and the rest of his crowd are drinking themselves into a frenzy. It was terrible."

"You think they mean trouble?"

She nodded slowly. "I believe they intend to handle things in their own way if they can."

"Have you told Kytros?"

She shook her head. "Apparently he went out just before I arrived."

Lomax got to his feet slowly, an unpleasant, crawling sensation in the pit of his stomach. "Things don't look so good, do they?"

"There are forty or fifty men waiting in the street outside," she said. "And more arriving every minute."

He slumped down on to the bed again, his mouth suddenly dry, and she took an automatic out of the pocket of her sheepskin jacket and handed it to him.

"I'm afraid it's rather old, but it's the best I could do."

His hand tightened over the worn butt and he frowned. "Are you suggesting I use this?"

"Is Dimitri Paros worth dying for?"

It was in that moment, knowing that she too believed he had killed Paros, that he realised just how hopeless the position was if he stayed.

"What have you got in mind?" he said. "Even if I overpower Stavrou, I can't just walk out of the front door. Is there a rear entrance?"

"Only a walled yard and others beyond that until finally you reach a narrow alley that brings you out further along the waterfront. I'll be waiting with the jeep by the town hall."

"It's dark, remember," he said. "I could easily lose my way."

She shook her head. "Not with Yanni to guide you. He's out there now."

"Then what happens?"

"Oliver and I have arranged things between us," she told him calmly. "All I have to do is get you to the villa. He'll have the launch ready for sea. You can be in Turkey in twelve hours. It's all quite simple, really."

For a moment he was going to tell her that nothing was ever that easy in life, that there was no place on top of earth where a murderer could run for cover, but there was no time. A step sounded in the corridor and the key turned in the lock.

Lomax started to get to his feet and Katina caught

hold of his sleeve. "Don't hurt him," she whispered. "He's a good man."

He nodded briefly and waited, the automatic held against his thigh. The door swung back against the wall and Stavrou came in.

"I'm sorry, Katina," he said. "You'll have to go now. If Kytros finds you here there'll be hell to pay."

In the same moment he turned to Lomax and looked into the barrel of the gun. His face turned pale and then his shoulders sagged. Quite suddenly, he seemed to have aged ten years.

He turned again to Katina and said bitterly, "You bitch. I'll lose my job over this."

"Do as I say and you won't get hurt," Lomax said. "Take off your tie and belt and lie face down on the bed."

Stavrou complied reluctantly and Lomax handed the gun to Katina and tied the man's wrists and ankles. For a gag, he used her headscarf.

They moved outside and he locked the cell and followed her through into the office. At the door, she paused and looked up at him without speaking. He held her hand tightly for a moment and then she went out and he locked the door behind her.

When he glanced through the slats of the shutters he could see the crowd scattered along the street in groups. He heard the voices and recognised the menace. Here were the beginnings of a mob. All they needed was a leader, someone with the courage to take them inside. He had an idea it wouldn't be long before one turned up.

He watched Katina drive away and then went along the corridor to the rear door. It was secured by two rusty bolts and he pulled them back with some difficulty and tried to open it. It still refused to budge and he slipped the automatic into his hip-pocket and worked his way through the half-dozen keys on the ring. The fourth one did the trick and he opened the door and moved cautiously ouside.

It was very still and he stood there for a moment waiting for his eyes to become accustomed to the dark before going forward.

The wall was perhaps twelve feet high. As he paused and looked up at it, a stone rattled under a shoe and Yanni appeared at his side.

"Over here, Mr. Lomax," he said. "There's an old olive tree growing in the corner."

"Good man." Lomax laid a hand lightly on his shoulder. "Let's get moving. We haven't got much time."

The boy went first and Lomax followed. The mortar between the stones had started to crumble, giving good footholds, and wedged between the olive tree and the wall he made quick progress. Within a few moments he was on top.

The boy led the way along several walls, finally dropping down into a timber yard. He crossed to a large double gate, opened a judas and peered outside. After a moment he nodded and went through the narrow opening.

They were standing in a stone-flagged alley which ran between high walls. It was a place of shadows, the only light a street lamp bracketed to the wall half-way along.

Yanni turned to speak. From somewhere in the darkness at the other end of the alley there was a movement and a voice cried in Greek. "He's escaping! The Englishman is escaping!"

At the same moment, two shots were fired so close that to any but the trained ear they might have sounded as one. Yanni started to run and Lomax jerked the automatic from his hip-pocket to return the fire. He pulled the trigger and the gun jammed.

Still clutching the useless weapon, he turned and ran, eyes fixed on the lamp half-way along the alley. Steps pounded over the flags behind him, the sound echoing from the walls. Again there was a shot and something whispered past his ear.

At that moment Yanni was passing under the lamp.

He turned to look back and Lomax hurled the automatic at the lamp, plunging the alley into darkness, and pushed him forward.

A moment later they reached the end of the alley and Yanni called breathlessly over his shoulder, "Careful, Mr. Lomax. We're back on the waterfront." He slowed to a trot and turned the corner straight into the arms of a burly fisherman.

He cursed angrily and grabbed the boy by the shirt. Lomax moved in fast, caught the man's right wrist and flung him against the wall, using his hip for leverage.

"Run for it, Yanni!" he said urgently and the boy darted across the road and disappeared into the shadows.

The fisherman lurched forward, great hands reaching out, and Lomax took a quick step back and kicked him in the stomach. As the man went down he became aware of confused shouting and turned to see that he was standing no more than fifty yards away from The Little Ship.

A truck was parked outside, the rear already packed with men, and others stood around it. Quite clearly in the light from the windows he saw Nikoli Aleko looking towards him. There was a sudden roar from the crowd as he was recognized and Lomax ran for his life.

He turned into the steeply shelving street that led to the square, his feet slipping on the cobbles, and behind him was aware of the deeper note of the truck's engine as it surged forward to meet the hill.

Voices rose on the night air, urging the driver on, and several men jumped to the ground and ran after him, able to make better time on the steep slope than the heavily laden truck.

Once he slipped and fell and a sound like hounds in full cry lifted into the night and then he was on his feet and running into the square.

Someone fired a shotgun. He ducked as pellets whistled through the air above his head and the jeep arrived on the scene, skidding broadside over the damp cobbles as Katina braked sharply.

She stood up, a rifle to her shoulder, and loosed off four shots that ricocheted from the ground in front of the truck, bringing it to a halt and sending those on foot diving for cover.

She waited for him, the collar of her sheepskin coat turned up, her face carved from stone, holding the Winchester sporting rifle with the telescopic sight. The gun he had given her that night at the farm so long ago.

He almost fell into the passenger seat and she handed him the Winchester and said calmly, "What about Yanni?"

"We ran into a little trouble," Lomax gasped, "but he's all right. For God's sake let's get out of here."

She gunned the motor and drove away very rapidly across the square. As they entered the narrow road that led out of town and across the bridge, another truck started to emerge. Lomax caught a brief glimpse of the driver's startled, frightened face before the man swung the wheel, crashing his vehicle into the wall and blocking the road.

Katina reversed quickly and started back across the square. The other truck had already breasted the hill and was moving rapidly to block the only remaining exit. The road to the other side of the island.

At the last moment, the driver braked to avoid a crash and Katina took the jeep through the dark, twisting street between the houses and out along the dirt road that led to the farm.

Whatever happened now, there was only one way they could reach the villa. Across the mountain and on foot.

16

The Run for Cover

They reached the farm a good five minutes in front of the truck and Katina braked to a halt in the yard beside the barn. Lomax got out and leaned over the trough to splash water on his face. When he raised his head, he saw that she was looking at him, a slight frown on her face.

"What is it?" he said.

"We stood together here once before," she replied slowly.

He nodded. "I remember."

She shivered slightly. "Is it then or now, Hugh?"

"I don't know, Katina," he said soberly. "Perhaps in some strange way each is a part of the other."

She reached out and took one of his hands and in that moment he knew with complete certainty that she was all he would ever want. He kissed her on the mouth and behind them the truck came over the rim of the hollow and started down towards the farm.

They crossed the yard, ducked under the fence and went up the slope through the olive trees. Katina led the way, moving expertly over the familiar ground in spite of the darkness.

Thunder rumbled ominously like gunfire in the distance, but otherwise a strange unnatural stillness hung over everything like a cloak. The truck came to a halt in the yard below, the engine was turned off and a door slammed.

Katina moved out of the shelter of the olive grove and

141

started across the bare hillside and Lomax followed her. At that moment, a bank of cloud rolled away from the moon, bathing everything in a hard white light.

A sudden cry sounded from below as they were seen and he turned and glanced down. He could see the truck quite clearly in the middle of the yard and the white faces of the men who looked up. Behind them, another truck was moving down the track to the farm.

Katina was already half-way across the barren hillside and he loosened the loop on the Winchester, slung it over his back and went after her.

It was a strange sensation to be hunted again and he was conscious of the old, familiar nervous excitement that crawled across his flesh and sharpened all the senses. He paused on the rim of a small plateau and looked down for a moment and saw the hunters already strung out in a ragged line as they moved up the hillside. Some of them carried lanterns and when the second truck came to a halt, he heard the excited barking of dogs.

A shot whined into the night, spending itself in space, hopelessly off target, and he stepped back so that he could no longer be seen.

Katina moved beside him, her face troubled. "Kytros can't be with them. He would never allow that."

Lomax wiped sweat from his brow with the back of one hand. "There's nothing to worry about. We've got a good start."

She shook her head. "Don't be too sure. Many of them are farmers and shepherds. They know the mountain. They can move across it at twice our speed."

Instead of working her way diagonally across the steep hillside, she went straight up, and Lomax followed her. The slope lifted steeply until it was almost perpendicular with rough tussocks of grass sticking out of the bare rock.

They came to the foot of an apron of loose stones and shale and she paused and glanced back over her shoulder.

"How are you making out?" she said anxiously as he joined her.

He managed a grin. "Let's say I'm not as young as I was."

"You must be careful from now on," she said. "The going is treacherous."

She started to climb, slowly and easily, testing every grass, every shrub, every rock, and Lomax followed her. After a while he forgot about the men who followed them, forgot about the danger as a strange exhilaration coursed through him.

Once, he heaved strongly on a boulder and it tore itself free and he swung quickly to one side. It bounced and crashed its way down the mountainside and the sound of it echoed away into the night.

There was a moment's breathless hush before Katina's voice drifted quietly down the slope. "Are you all right?"

"Only just," he called back softly, and started to climb again.

A moment later the ground sloped away and he found himself standing on the edge of a broad plateau. He turned and gazed down into the shadows of the valley, but could see no sign of their pursuers.

Katina moved beside him. "They have taken the easy way over," she said. "Remember the track we used on that first night when I guided you to the villa?"

"And where do we go from here?" Lomax said.

She turned and pointed across the plateau to the great rock wall that faced them. It was splashed with moonlight, fissures and cracks branching across it like dark fingers, and Lomax whistled softly. "Are you sure it can be done?"

She nodded. "Oh, yes, I climbed it several times as a girl. It isn't anything like as formidable as it looks."

She looked up at him anxiously and he grinned. "We don't have much choice, do we?"

She turned and led the way across the plateau, picking

her way between great boulders. When they reached the base of the rock Lomax saw that it wasn't actually perpendicular, but tilted back slightly in great slabs, most of which were split and fissured into a thousand cracks.

Katina started to climb at once and Lomax followed her. He didn't look down until he had climbed forty or fifty feet. For a moment he appeared to be floating in space and a giant hand seemed to be trying to pull him away from the face of the rock. He breathed deeply and closed his eyes. When he opened them again, everything was all right.

He didn't look down after that, but climbed steadily and strongly. Five minutes later, he came over the edge of a wide ledge which was partly sheltered by an uptilted slab and found Katina waiting for him.

"Are you all right?" she said.

Now that he had stopped climbing, he was conscious that his limbs were trembling slightly, but he nodded confidently. "Are we stopping here?"

She shook her head. "We can't afford the time. Even this way, we'll be lucky to reach the temple before the best of the mountain men using the track."

She started to climb again quickly. Lomax followed her, trying to forget his aching limbs, concentrating on the rock, and a wind moved in from the sea, cutting through the woollen sweater, and thunder rumbled again, but much nearer this time.

He moved over the edge of the last great tilted slab of rock and found Katina waiting for him. Above them a perpendicular wall of rock lifted a hundred feet into the night and Lomax craned his neck, gazing up at it, the sweat on his face beginning to dry in the cold wind.

She turned and indicated a dark chimney that cut its way straight through the solid rock to the top of the cliff. "It looks bad, but it's the easiest part of the climb."

He found it an effort to smile. "I'll take your word for it."

He waited until she had disappeared into the darkness above him before following. He hung the Winchester around his neck and used the common mountaineering technique, bracing his back against one wall and feet against the other, resting every fifteen or twenty feet, his body firmly wedged.

After a while, he found that it was possible to climb properly and the handholds were good and plentiful. Ten minutes later he scrambled over the edge and joined Katina.

They stood on the rim of the main plateau at the top of the mountain and the temple and tomb of Achilles were three hundred yards to the rear. Below them the whole of the south side of the island swept down through moonlight into the sea.

It was an incredible sight, but Lomax was still conscious of that unnatural stillness and a blanket of dark moved in fast from the horizon, blotting out the stars as it came.

Thunder sounded overhead and Katina said, "The storm should break soon. It will give us good cover on the way down."

They started forward and there was a faint cry, carried on the wind from somewhere on their right. Lomax turned as three men emerged over the far rim of the plateau accompanied by two hounds. They were no more than two hundred yards away and clearly visible in the bright moonlight.

He raised the Winchester and fired once and one of the hounds jumped into the air and disappeared over the edge.

"That should hold them for a while." He pushed Katina forward. "Let's get out of here."

They ran towards the temple, Katina leading the way. When Lomax turned and glanced towards the right, he saw that the three men and the other dog were moving very fast on a parallel course with the obvious intention of intercepting them. One of them was a good fifty yards in front of his companions and gaining steadily. A moment later they all disappeared behind a slight rise.

Lomax followed Katina between great boulders, slipping and sliding over the rough ground, and mounted the steps to the terrace. As they started across the mosaic floor between the pillars, Nikoli Aleko emerged from the shadows on their right and ran towards them.

The black eye-patch stood out prominently against his face and his teeth were bared in a savage grin. He carried a gutting knife in his right hand and the blade gleamed dully.

Lomax pushed Katina violently to one side and met him on the run. As the knife came up, he parried it with the barrel of the Winchester and swung the butt against the unprotected jaw. Aleko staggered back into a pillar without a sound and rolled on to his face.

As Lomax went down the slope to the hollow, there was a tremendous clap of thunder. Rain began to fall as he moved past the shepherd's hut and started to follow Katina across the treacherous apron of shale and loose earth that spilled down three or four hundred feet through the great, sloping ravine.

When she reached the half-way mark, she paused and glanced back and her foot slipped. She dug in her heels desperately and a ripple seemed to pass over the surface of the shale. Lomax kept on going and a moment later they were together.

By now the rain had increased into a torrential downpour that drowned all sound. He leaned close and nodded encouragingly and then a tremendous sheet of lightning momentarily turned night into day and her mouth opened in a soundless scream.

He swung round. On the rim of the hollow no more than twenty yards away stood Aleko's two companions and the remaining dog. In the same instant, the animal sprang out into space.

As it landed, Lomax struck out wildly with the Winchester and the whole earth seemed to move beneath him. He was conscious of Katina's cry of alarm and the snarling of the dog and then they were all sliding down through the ravine on a great wave of earth and shale.

He dropped the Winchester and clawed at the slope with both hands, but it was too late. For a terrible moment he seemed to ride the wind through the darkness and the rain and then the movement slowed as the ravine levelled out.

He heard Katina calling to him through the darkness and went sliding down the slope to join her. She was standing beside a large boulder in two feet of water and he reached out for her anxiously. "Are you all right?"

She fell against him, her arms sliding around his neck. "I thought I was never going to stop."

"At least we've come a long way down in a hell of a short time," he said. "We'd better take advantage of it."

As he finished speaking, shale and loose earth showered down on them and the dog snarled somewhere above. It erupted from the darkness and landed with a splash about six feet away.

Lomax pushed Katina to one side and picked up a large stone in his two hands and brought it down with all his force as the animal surged forward. There was a terrible cracking sound and the hound gave a strange, whimpering cry and fell to one side, thrashing the water.

Lomax turned away, sobbing for breath. He took Katina by one arm and together they scrambled over the slippery boulders and up out of the pool. A moment later they were moving down the side of the mountain through the heavy rain.

17

Confessional

When they reached the villa Katina was limping heavily and Lomax supported her as they climbed out of the ditch and crossed the road.

The gates stood open and the lamp suspended from the archway above swayed in the wind, a pool of light constantly reaching into the darkness and retreating again.

They moved along the narrow flagged path between the olive trees and the rain seemed to drown all sound. Lomax was soaked to the skin, dark hair plastered across his forehead. Every muscle in his body ached and he found it an effort to place one foot in front of the other.

Katina was almost at breaking point, nerve and sinew stretched to the limit. She stumbled as they came to the edge of the trees and he caught her in his arms.

He held her very close and said softly, "Not long now. It's almost over."

And then he heard the sound of the piano as he had heard it once before in this place, nostalgic and wistful. He was trapped again at the crossing point between the present and the past and he stood there in the rain holding the girl, the music filling him with a strange, aching sadness.

The french window was ajar, one end of a red velvet curtain billowing into the rain as a gust of wind lifted it. Katina pulled it back and they moved inside.

A log fire burned on the wide stone hearth and the room was illuminated by the lamp that stood on the piano. In its light, Van Horn's hair gleamed like silver.

He was wearing a smoking jacket in corded green silk and he jumped up and came forward, a frown on his face.

"I thought you were never coming. What happened?"

At that moment Katina sighed and started to slide to the floor. Lomax caught her in his arms and carried her across to the divan.

Van Horn sat beside her, rolled back an eyelid with his thumb and took her pulse. After a moment he looked up. "She's completely exhausted. Get the brandy. It's in the cupboard under the bookshelves."

Lomax found the bottle and two glasses and returned. He filled one and gave it to Van Horn and used the other himself.

The liquid burned its way down into his stomach and he filled his glass again and watched Van Horn raise Katina's head and force open her mouth. She choked and started to cough and then her eyes opened.

She tried to sit up and Van Horn said, "It's all right, my dear. You're at the villa."

She stared blankly at him and then something clicked in her eyes. "Is the boat ready?"

He nodded and she swung her legs to the floor. "Then what are we sitting here for?"

She tried to stand up and Lomax pushed her down. "There's no hurry, Katina," he said. "Not any more. I'm not going anywhere."

She stared up at him, a slight, puzzled frown on her face, and Van Horn said, "Don't be a fool, Lomax. I heard you'd accused Alexias of murdering Dimitri Paros, but you haven't a hope in hell of proving it."

Lomax helped himself to a cigarette from the silver box on top of the piano. He lit it slowly and blew out a long column of smoke. He felt very tired and there was a slight, persistent ache just behind his right eye.

"But I don't think it was Alexias who murdered Dimitri," he said softly. "I think it was you."

Thunder rumbled again and the rain increased in a sudden rush, hammering against the window. There was no change of expression on Van Horn's face. He said calmly, "Are you quite sure you know what you're saying?"

Katina stood up and moved forward, her eyes very large in the white face. "What are you trying to suggest, Hugh?"

He placed his hands gently on her shoulders. "Someone tried to kill me in the alley at the back of the prison tonight. Someone who knew I was coming out. And the automatic you gave me. For some strange reason it wouldn't fire."

She looked up at him, horror in her eyes, and he went on, "Did Van Horn know that your uncle played chess with Father John Mikali every Thursday night?"

She nodded. "Everybody knows."

"Then why didn't he tell me I was wasting my time when I said I intended visiting your uncle?"

She turned slowly and looked at Van Horn and Lomax went on, "When I got to the farm, Dimitri and the Samos brothers were waiting for me in the dark. There was only one possible explanation. Dimitri was expecting me because someone had warned him I was coming. But only one person knew."

Van Horn smiled lightly. "It doesn't even hang together. How on earth could I have got in touch with him in time? Katina took the jeep."

It was Katina who answered him. "You were on the telephone to someone when I came up from the kitchen and Dimitri worked most nights at The Little Ship. Everyone knew that."

Van Horn lit a cigarette, his hand as steady as a rock. "You still haven't placed me at the farm at the time of the murder. No jury in the world would accept for one moment that a man of my age and condition could cross the mountain twice on the same night within a matter of hours."

"That worried me for a while," Lomax said. "Until I remembered Katina once telling me there was a jetty at the bottom of the cliffs near the farm." He glanced down at her. "How long would you say it would take from here to there by sea?"

"Twenty minutes," she said. "I've done it often. So has Oliver."

Lomax looked enquiringly at Van Horn. "Would you care to guarantee the launch hasn't been to sea tonight? We could always check."

"You're not making sense," Van Horn said. "What possible motive could I have had for killing Dimitri Paros?"

"It's only a guess, but I'd say he'd discovered you were the man responsible for the death of his father," Lomax said.

Katina's breath hissed sharply between her teeth. For a moment Van Horn's composure almost broke, but he rallied strongly. "It won't do, Lomax. Everyone knows what I went through at Fonchi."

"When we were discussing things earlier today, I told you I thought Alexias Pavlo was the traitor," Lomax said. "You pointed out that I still had to explain how the Germans got on to him in the first place. I can do better than that. I can show how they got on to you."

"I'm afraid you're not making sense," Van Horn said, but all colour had left his face and deep lines were scoured across his forehead.

"When I first visited this house seventeen years ago, Joe Boyd borrowed a volume of your war poems called *The Survivor*," Lomax told him. "It was bound in green leather and autographed in gold, one of a complete edition of your works."

He went to the bookshelves and returned with a slim green volume which he dropped on the coffee table. "The book in question. I noticed it earlier when Katina brought me up from the hotel to meet you again. It wasn't until tonight that I realised it had no business being there."

"I don't understand," Katina said.

"I think Van Horn does. You see Joe Boyd forgot to return the book. He was carrying it in one of his tunic pockets when he went into action. I only remembered that tonight after all these years. The Germans must have found it when they searched his body. No wonder I thought Steiner was laughing at me when I told him we hadn't been in contact with anyone on the island."

Van Horn picked up the book and examined it. After a while, he sighed. "It would have been a pity to spoil the set. It was presented to me by my American publishers just before the war."

He crossed to the bookshelves, replaced the volume then took a decanter from the cupboard and poured himself a drink. When he spoke, his voice sounded curiously remote. It was almost as if he were discussing something that had happened to someone else.

"You're right, of course. They found the book and Steiner came straight to me. I tried to beat about the bush, but it didn't do any good."

Katina moved forward, dragging her right foot slightly. "Why did you tell them?"

He tried to turn away, but she caught his arm and pulled him round to face her. "Why, Oliver?"

He shrugged. "Because I was afraid. He threatened to send me to Gestapo headquarters in Athens."

"Was that all?"

Van Horn shook his head. "No, he swore he'd destroy every piece in my collection. He smashed the amphora just to show me he meant business."

She turned away, loathing on her face, and Lomax said, "Why did Steiner keep you in the town gaol instead of sending you to Fonchi with the others?"

"Your apparent death on the way to Crete made a convenient scapegoat," Van Horn told him. "Steiner was going to release me after six months on the grounds of my health."

"So that you could inform on more of your friends?" Katina asked.

He ignored her and went on, "Unfortunately, Steiner was killed and his replacement knew nothing of the arrangement. He had me transferred to Fonchi soon after taking over command."

"So you condemned your friends to a hell on earth because you were afraid," Katina said. "Because of your stupid collection."

"I suffered as much as anyone," he said. "You've seen what they did to me, Lomax. When you told me you suspected Alexias, that you intended to have a showdown with him, I panicked. I knew you were bound to turn something up if you dug around for long enough."

"So you got in touch with Dimitri?"

Van Horn nodded. "He said he'd take care of things, but insisted on seeing me. I went in the launch as you guessed. When I arrived, he was drunk. Apparently he'd put two-and-two together."

"And you realised he intended to blackmail you?"

"There was a gutting knife on the table. I thought that if I used that, it would make Kytros think the murderer was a fisherman."

"Rather an unusual way to stab a man."

Van Horn shrugged. "A trick I learned in the trenches. One never really forgets how to do that sort of thing. You should know that better than most people."

Lomax ignored the thrust. "And the business in the alley at the back of the prison? I was right about that?"

Van Horn nodded. "When Katina came out to the villa and asked me to help you get out, I couldn't very well refuse. The automatic I gave her had a damaged firing pin, by the way. After she'd left in the jeep, I followed her into town on an old bicycle we've had in the stables for years."

Lomax was beginning to feel tired and the pain in his head was worse. "So you killed?" he said. "And made me kill? And for what, Van Horn? To what end?"

"I don't know," Van Horn said. "I really don't. Is there ever an end to anything?"

He put his right hand into his pocket and produced a revolver. Katina took a quick step backwards and Lomax said, "More killing, Van Horn? But you won't be able to stop with me. What about Katina? Will you shoot her also?"

"I don't think so," a familiar voice said, and Kytros stepped in through the french window, Alexias Pavlo at his shoulder.

Van Horn's eyes flickered towards them and Lomax shoved Katina to one side and jumped. He was too late by a mile. Van Horn fired at point-blank range and the heavy bullet caught Lomax in the right shoulder, smashing him back against the piano.

As Katina screamed, his arm swung against the lamp, knocking it sideways, plunging the room into darkness as he slid to the floor.

18

Dust and Ashes

For a few moments there was only the darkness and its confusion and Lomax was conscious of Katina beside him. When the main lights were turned on, there was no sign of Van Horn or Alexias. Kytros moved from the switch to the door which led to the hall, but it refused to open.

He turned and said calmly, "He won't get far. I took the precaution of locking the main gates when we arrived and Stavrou is guarding the cliff path."

Lomax reached for the edge of the piano to pull himself up and Katina moved to help him. The wound in his shoulder was bleeding steadily and she quickly made a thick pad of an embroidered table-runner and pushed it inside his sweater. Kytros came forward. "Is it bad?"

Lomax shook his head. "I'll survive. How long were you on the terrace?"

"Long enough—not that it made any difference." Kytros smiled slightly. "I knew before I got here. I told you I was waiting for Doctor Spanos to finish his autopsy. He came up with two most interesting points."

"I don't understand," Lomax said.

"In the first place, Dimitri Paros had been dead for longer than we supposed. The fact that his body was so close to the fire had delayed rigor mortis."

"And the second point?"

"The dead man had smashed his wrist-watch when falling. It had stopped at exactly nine o'clock." Kytros sighed. "You must forgive a simple island policeman for failing to notice the fact sooner."

"And at nine o'clock I was at sea with the Samos brothers."

"And Alexias was playing chess with Father John."

"But what put you on to Van Horn?"

"In the first place, simple logic," Kytros said. "Riki Samos admitted that Dimitri had been tipped off that you were going to the farm, but he didn't know by whom. From what you had told me earlier, it seemed that only one person could be responsible. I then discovered that Dimitri had left The Little Ship after receiving a telephone call and there are very few on the island."

"And the operator remembered who'd called him?"

Kytros nodded. "I stopped to pick up Alexias and heard you were on the loose. Then Yanni turned up at the police station considerably distressed because he thought you were going to be torn to pieces on the mountain."

"And you didn't?" Lomax said.

Kytros permitted himself a slight smile. "I considered it unlikely in view of your past history in these islands."

"Something else to thank Yanni for," Katina said.

Kytros nodded. "A good boy. A pity there is no one to educate him."

"I think that could be arranged," Lomax said.

A shot echoed flatly through the rain outside and Alexias moved in from the terrace. "He's in the garden," he said harshly.

Kytros unbuckled his holster and took out his automatic. "I think it would be better if you remained here."

He crossed to the window and Lomax moved after him. Outside, the rain lanced down through the light that spilled across the terrace to the bushes and beyond was darkness.

There was another revolver shot followed by the dry, ominous rattle of a machine pistol. "Stavrou!" Kytros said, and he ran across the terrace and plunged into the garden.

Faintly through the rain came the sound of many voices and the barking of dogs and Katina touched Lomax's arm and pointed. In the darkness on the other side of the road, men moved down the slope towards the villa, their lanterns like eyes in the night.

In the garden all was silent and obeying a sudden impulse Lomax ran across the terrace clutching his shoulder and plunged into the undergrowth. He crouched beside a bush, the rain falling on him, and Katina arrived a moment later. "This is madness," she protested.

He moved forward cautiously between the dripping olive trees without replying, and above them on the mountainside the noise grew louder and more ominous.

Kytros stepped from behind a tree to join them. Before he could speak there was a movement in the bushes on the other side of the garden and the machine pistol rattled again. Stavrou shouted something unintelligible and Van Horn ran headlong out of the undergrowth, left arm raised to protect his face.

He lurched against a tree and stood there staring at them, his breath a white mist in the damp air. In the yellow lamplight, his skin had turned to parchment and he looked old and tired and defeated.

He turned and staggered along the drive towards the main gate. As he reached it, the mob poured down from the mountain and flooded across the road.

Lomax and Katina paused and Alexias came up behind them and there was a strange silence. It was as if, somehow, the people outside the gate realised that something extraordinary was taking place.

Stavrou emerged from the trees and waited, the barrel of his machine pistol pointed towards the gate. Kytros nodded to him and moved forward on his own. When he paused, legs slightly apart, he was holding the automatic against his right thigh.

"Throw down your gun, Mr. Van Horn," he said. "Let no one else suffer in this business."

Van Horn started to raise the revolver, almost in slow motion, his finger tightening on the trigger. In the same moment Kytros flung his arm forward and fired. The heavy slug pushed Van Horn back against the gate and the crowd scattered hurriedly.

He reached backwards, grasping one of the iron bars with his left hand to hold himself upright. Very deliberately, he raised the gun again, and Kytros shot him twice in the body.

There was a terrible groan from the crowd and Van Horn slithered to the ground, hands folded across his stomach as the life spilled out of him.

He looked up as Lomax went forward and tried to speak. A moment later, he started to choke and blood gushed from his mouth in a bright stream.

Beyond the gate the crowd were quiet in the rain, not yet understanding what had taken place, waiting for someone to explain. Alexias moved beside Lomax looking old and tired as if all at once life had become too much for him. He tried to find words, but none would come and he went towards the gate.

Kytros unlocked it and Alexias passed outside and started to speak quietly to the crowd and the sergeant dropped to one knee beside Van Horn and examined the body.

After a moment, he looked up and said calmly, "There is no blame here for you, Mr. Lomax. This man wished to die. He made me kill him."

Lomax stood there clutching his arm, feeling the blood ooze between his fingers, and the lamp above the gate seemed to grow to enormous proportions. He turned and went along the drive to the villa.

The front door stood open to the night and he passed through the hall and the narrow, whitewashed passage and came into the great glass room containing Van Horn's ceramics.

The showcases seemed to be suspended in the night, circling the great red and black amphora that floated, disembodied, in the darkness.

He stood there, staring at it, sweat on his face, and a spasm of blind, unreasoning rage surged up inside him. He lurched forward and pushed it sideways from the plinth with his good arm, sending it smashing in a thousand pieces across the floor. And then, for some unaccountable reason, he failed to catch his breath and night moved in on him as great dry sobs tore at his throat.

He went out on the balcony, and somehow Katina was beside him, and he said brokenly, "Dust and ashes, Katina. Dust and ashes."

"I know, Hugh," she said simply.

He stood at the rail and looked out on beauty. The rain had stopped and the freshness of wet earth hung on the damp air and he was alive.

After a while, he slid his good arm around her shoulders and they went back into the house.